棋 王

THE CHESS MASTER

D1559857

中國現代文學中英對照系列
Bilingual Series on Modern Chinese Literature

棋 王
The Chess Master

中英對照版
Chinese-English Bilingual Edition

阿城 著

詹納爾 英譯

Original Chinese Text by
A CHENG
Translated by W.J.F. Jenner

The Chinese University Press

出 版 人 的 話

　　近二十年，中國與外界接觸日趨頻繁，影響所及，華文作家在世界文學圈中益受注目。二〇〇〇年諾貝爾文學獎由高行健先生獲得，或非偶然。

　　中文大學出版社一向秉承促進中西方文化交流的使命，故於年前開始籌劃「中國現代文學中英對照系列」，邀得鄭樹森教授出任編輯委員會主席，及幾位國際著名學者出任成員，挑選中國著名作家之重要作品及現有之最佳英譯本，以中英文雙語對照排列出版，計劃每年出書五至六種。個別名作亦會另邀翻譯界高手操刀。各書均邀學界專家特撰新序，以為導讀。

　　本社謹對編輯委員會及各界友人之鼎力協助，致以熱切謝忱。

Publisher's Note

It is a recent phenomenon that authors of Chinese origin have been attracting more international attention in the literary world, probably as a result of China's increasing cultural interactions with the outside world in the past two decades. As such, it was not coincidental that the 2000 Nobel Prize was awarded to Gao Xingjian, an author of Chinese origin.

With the mission to bridge the gap between Chinese and Western cultures, The Chinese University Press is uniquely situated to play an active role in this area. Thus, this *Bilingual Series on Modern Chinese Literature* has come into existence. Under the able guidance of Professor William Tay and other members of the Advisory Committee, it is planned that five to six titles will be added to the list annually. They will be important works by major authors and will be presented in a bilingual format for cross-cultural appreciation. This means the Committee has either to identify the best existing translations, or to commission experts who can do the job equally well. Each author in the series will also be introduced by a noted scholar in the field to put the work in a critical perspective.

The publisher appreciates the invaluable advice of the Advisory Committee, and sincerely thanks all those who have helped to make this series a reality.

Contents

目 錄

Introduction

Ngai Ling-tun

Ph.D., Department of East Asian Languages & Literature
University of Wisconsin-Madison, U.S.A.

*I think the Chinese at play are much more lovable than the Chinese
in business. Whereas the Chinese in politics are ridiculous and in
society are childish, at leisure they are at their best. They have so
much leisure and so much leisurely joviality.*

Lin Yutang

I

The discerning reader may find A Cheng's (b. Zhong Acheng, 1949–)
"The Chess Master" (1984) familiar. In fact, he may even have a vague
sense of *déjà lu*. This is partly due to the specific references in the story
to Honoré de Balzac's novella *Cousin Pons* and Jack London's short
story "Love of Life", or the sentiments akin to those expressed in Knut
Hamsun's works, as suggested by Bonnie S. McDougall. But more
importantly, it is the affinities in plot, characterisation, narrative point
of view and thematic concerns between A Cheng's story and Stefan
Zweig's (1881–1942) "The Royal Game" (1942) that give the reader
such an impression.

Like "The Royal Game", "The Chess Master" begins with a scene
of passengers boarding, filled with the hustle and bustle prior to
departure. The main action of "The Royal Game" takes place on an

導　論

危令敦

美國威斯康辛大學麥迪遜校區

東亞語言文學系博士

> 我想中國人在玩耍尋樂的時候，比之幹正經事情的時
> 候遠為可愛。中國人上政治舞台，荒誕不經，進了社會，
> 稚態可掬，空閒的時候，方是最純良的時候。他們有那麼
> 許多空閒，又有那麼許多空閒的興致。
>
> 　　　　　　　　　　　　　　　　　　　　林語堂

　　　　　　　　　　　　一

　　明眼的讀者可能覺得阿城(原名鍾阿城，1949-)的〈棋王〉(1984)似曾相識，甚至依稀有讀過的感覺。究其原因，可能與此篇小說談到巴爾扎克的中篇小說《邦斯舅舅》和傑克‧倫敦的短篇小說〈熱愛生命〉有關。再者，一如杜博妮所說，此篇小說所表達的思想感情與克努特‧哈姆孫的作品相近，這也可能是原因之一。但更重要的是，阿城的小說與斯蒂芬‧茨威格(1881–1942)的〈象棋的故事〉(1942)無論在情節、人物塑造、敘述角度，以及主題關懷各方面均有共通之處，所以讀者才會有這種印象。

　　〈棋王〉和〈象棋的故事〉同樣以亂哄哄的送別場面為小說拉開序幕。〈象棋的故事〉的主要情節在一艘從紐約開往布宜諾斯艾利斯的輪船上展開，〈棋王〉的故事則始於火車上，終於中國的鄉間。兩篇

ocean liner voyaging from New York to Buenos Aires, while the story of "The Chess Master" unfolds on a train preparing for departure from a city and subsequently in the countryside of China. Both stories involve characters that are away from home. In "The Royal Game", Mirko Czentovic, the world champion of European chess from Yugoslavia, is on his way to an exhibition tour in Argentina. Aboard the same ship is Dr. B, an obscure chess player fleeing from Austria, which was then under Nazi occupation. Wang Yisheng, the young hero of "The Chess Master", leaves his hometown for a different reason. Like most of the high school students in the story, he is responding to Chairman Mao Zedong's call in 1968 to settle down in the countryside and learn from the peasants. It is in the first scene that the narrators of both stories get to know their main characters.

In both stories, there are two episodes in which the main characters' talent for chess is shown. Czentovic is an orphan of peasant stock. Raised by a pastor who happens to love chess, he has the opportunity to learn the art of the checkered board by observation. One day the pastor discovers Czentovic's talent for chess. He drives him to a nearby town where good chess players reside and challenges them to a contest with Czentovic. Quite unexpectedly, the novice defeats them one by one with ease. The episode culminates in the final game, which is organised on the next day in a chess club for the chess fanatic Count Simczic. In this game, Czentovic has to play against several contestants at the same time and stuns everyone by winning seven of the eight games. Convinced of Czentovic's gift for chess, Count Simczic offers to support him by paying for his professional training.

However, to find out whether Czentovic is a great chess player, the reader has to wait until the second chess match. This takes place on the ocean liner, when Czentovic, now a world champion, takes on a group of amateurs for money. Czentovic slays them in the first game, and accepts their second challenge. It is at this juncture that Dr. B

小說所描寫的角色，都是離家在外的人。在〈象棋的故事〉裏，米爾柯‧琴多維奇乃南斯拉夫國手，國際象棋的世界冠軍，正乘船南下阿根廷，展開他的表演之旅。同船的還有乙博士，這位寂寂無名的棋手剛逃離納粹佔領的奧地利。〈棋王〉的年輕主角王一生，則為了完全不同的原因而離開他原來生活的城市。他和小說裏大部分的高中生一樣，是為了響應毛主席1968年發出的「上山下鄉」的號召而到農村去的。兩篇小說的敘述者同樣在小說的第一幕裏結識主人公。

兩篇小說同樣安排了兩場棋賽來表現主要人物的棋藝。琴多維奇出身農家，幼失怙恃，由牧師養大。牧師愛下棋，琴多維奇得以旁觀學藝。後來牧師發現他有這方面的天分，於是將他帶到棋手薈萃的鄰鎮，一會各方高人。想不到這位初出道的毛頭小子竟不費吹灰之力，便將對手逐一擊敗。此段插曲的高潮是翌日象棋俱樂部裏的車輪大戰：在特意為棋癡西姆奇茨老伯爵舉辦的比賽裏，琴多維奇以一敵八，贏了七人，技驚四座。老伯爵驚為天人，當即慷慨解囊，資助琴多維奇拜師學藝。

琴多維奇的棋藝是否精湛，讀者必須待到第二場比賽，方才知曉。此時的琴多維奇已非吳下阿蒙，而是堂堂的世界冠軍。在船上，他為了金錢而與一群業餘愛好者下棋。他輕易的贏了第一局，並同意再下一盤。此時乙博士現身，助烏合之眾一臂之力。乙博士

appears and lends the amateurs a hand. He surprises the group—and the reader as well—with his uncanny ability to foresee many moves ahead. No sooner have the dazzled amateurs collected themselves than the game ends in a draw. The excited amateurs can hardly wait to arrange for a re-match between Dr. B and Czentovic on the following day. This time Czentovic loses the first game, but wins the second by adopting a very simple strategy. Aware of Dr. B's nimble mind, Czentovic torments him with deliberate delaying tactics. As the game drags on, Dr. B begins to lose his patience with Czentovic. He becomes so absorbed in his own calculations that he ignores the game altogether, and eventually loses it. What the world champion and the onlookers do not know is that Dr. B has a pathological history of obsessive compulsion which is caused mainly by his fixation with chess. If the perceptive narrator has not intervened in time, Dr. B would have probably relapsed into hysteria again. Despite his defeat in the second game, Dr. B seems to be a better chess player and have the potential to be a great player. Yet in the end, no real chess master emerges.

In comparison, the first episode of a chess match in A Cheng's story is rather uneventful. It takes place on the state farm where the narrator works, when the chess addict Wang Yisheng comes to visit him. Knowing that Wang is good at playing Chinese chess, those students working at the farm rush to invite their best player Ni Bin over for a chess match. Ni comes from a notable family in southern China. His ancestor is none other than Ni Zan, the famous painter, calligrapher and poet of the Yuan Dynasty. Moreover, according to Ni Bin, Ni Zan was also a great chess player, and there is a long tradition of chess playing in the family. In sharp contrast to Ni, Wang is an orphan from a poor family. His background is very similar to that of Czentovic. He learns chess from an old garbage collector who happens to own an ancient chess anthology of a very obscure origin. Wang and Ni are so good at the game that they decide to play blind, leaving the enthusiastic

運籌畫策，佔盡先機，令眾人——還有讀者——不勝詫異；耳迷目眩的業餘棋手尚未反應過來，雙方已經和棋了。眾人喜不自禁，連忙為兩大高手安排第二天的重賽。這一次比賽，琴多維奇先輸一局，然後贏第二局。他取勝的秘訣很簡單：乙博士心思敏捷，他便以慢制快。比賽一拖拉，乙博士就失去耐性，並漸漸墮入自己設想的棋局裏，完全無視眼前的比賽，終至敗北。琴多維奇和觀眾並不曉得，原來乙博士因為沉迷象棋，導致心神耗損，曾經有過精神崩潰的病歷。若不是敘述者察言觀色，及時阻止乙博士繼續比賽，他實有舊病復發之虞。乙博士雖然輸了一局，可是棋藝似在琴多維奇之上，而且甚有大將之風，可謂雖敗猶榮。可惜故事終了，讀者依然不曉得誰是真正的棋王。

相較之下，〈棋王〉的第一場對弈便顯得平平無奇。棋呆子王一生到敘述者工作的農場看他，結果遇上對手。知青都知道王一生的象棋棋藝了得，趕緊請來隊裏最佳棋手倪斌，與他比試。倪斌乃南方名門之後，祖上是元代大名鼎鼎的畫家、書法家和詩人倪雲林。據倪斌所言，倪雲林還是棋壇名手，所以家裏素有下棋的傳統。王一生的身世自然難與倪斌比較：他出身寒門，而且父母雙亡，與琴多維奇頗為相似。他的棋藝，傳自一拾荒老人；而老人的棋道，則悟自一本古代異書。王一生與倪斌棋逢對手，乾脆下起盲棋，眾人

spectators at a loss. Although no one is able to follow their moves, the onlookers can tell in the end that Ni yields the palm to Wang. This is the first indication of Wang's fathomless skills.

Wang's real talent as a chess master is fully dramatised in the second episode, when Ni introduces him, about six months later, to the second-place and third-place winners of a local tournament that has just finished in a small town, and challenges them to a contest with Wang. As the news gets out, more players volunteer to play against Wang, including the champion. In the end Wang has to play a multiple game blind, against nine contestants at the same time. This is indeed one of the most captivating scenes in the story, manifestly far more compelling than Czentovic's first game. Though a little shaken, Wang manages to defeat them, one by one; until the last opponent, the champion, shows up in person and asks for a draw. The champion turns out to be a suave and sophisticated old man from a respectable family. To save the worthy opponent's face, Wang gracefully agrees. In a manner reminiscent of Czentovic's remarkable feats, Wang wins eight out of nine games. Similarly, the Chinese king of chess is crowned in the end by the champion, whose social standing is similar to Count Simczic's.

Wang Yisheng is a character with humble origin like Czentovic, but also with the intellectual capacity of Dr. B. Insofar as chess is concerned, one may even say that Wang possesses the best qualities of Czentovic and Dr. B, such as the former's persistence and composure, and the latter's exuberant imagination and nimble mind. Yet Wang seems to have none of the weaknesses. Whereas Czentovic is intellectually handicapped and unable to play blind, Wang is so gifted that he is able to play blind against multiple opponents simultaneously. In terms of ability to calculate, Wang also seems superior to Dr. B, despite the fact that Dr. B is a much better educated person. Furthermore, Wang possesses positive qualities such as moral

看不明白，只有乾納悶兒。儘管如此，大家後來還是知道王一生贏了。此段插曲裏，王一生牛刀小試，已技驚四座。

好戲在後頭，王一生的棋藝要到第二次比賽才見真章。六個月後，經倪斌引見，王一生得以結識鎮上剛奪地區象棋比賽的亞軍和季軍，並一較高下。消息傳出，更多棋手請纓加入，冠軍也不甘後人，報名比試。結果王一生要以一敵九，下的是盲棋。此為小説裏最為扣人心弦的一段，比琴多維奇的首役實在精彩得多。王一生有點忐忑不安，不過還能沉着應戰，並將對手逐一擊潰，直至最後一名強手──是次比賽的冠軍──現身求和為止。冠軍原來是一名溫文爾雅的老人，乃山區世家後人。王一生識英雄重英雄，遂同意言和。王一生九戰八勝，大有琴多維奇力克群雄之風。中華棋王之加冕，亦同樣由身份和地位猶如西姆奇茨老伯爵之世家後人來完成。

王一生的出身與琴多維奇相同，智力則與乙博士相近。就棋道而言，王一生可謂集二人之長處於一身：他像琴多維奇那樣堅定沉着，同時擁有乙博士的非凡想像與敏捷的心思。可是王一生並沒有他們的弱點。琴多維奇天資不足，無法下盲棋，王一生卻有同時下九盤盲棋的異稟。乙博士的學養雖然比他好，可是王一生神機妙算，預見能力似乎猶勝乙博士一籌。除此之外，王一生還有情操高

integrity and inner strength. The hand-to-mouth existence does not drive him in search of material gain and fame, which contrasts sharply with Czentovic's vulgar greed and lust for rank. Wang's refusal to accept Ni Bin's bribing of the officials in order to enter him into the chess tournament provides further evidence of his uprightness. Wang's inner strength is equally impressive, especially when compared with Dr. B. It is particularly evident in the marathon of the multiple game. For A Cheng, Wang's single-minded obsession with chess would by no means jeopardise his mental health. The ordeal of playing against nine contestants only serves to enlighten the semi-literate master with the meaning of spiritual sustenance, which he has never taken seriously before. On top of that, his willingness to settle for a draw with the champion shows his modesty and magnanimity—indeed a strong contrast to Czentoivc's arrogance and Dr. B's craving for victory. In A Cheng's story, an ordinary man is not necessarily ordinary. He could be a person of intelligence and inner strength. Once inspired, he can rise to the occasion and transcend himself against all odds.

In both stories, chess is at first perceived by the narrators as a diversion to relieve stress and anxiety in a harsh and hostile environment. The protagonists' fixation on chess stems from a strong desire to resist or escape from an unpleasant world. Dr. B gets to learn chess while he is under house arrest by the Gestapo. The unbearable void of his incarceration prompts him to seize at anything that can stimulate his mental energy. The passage describing his thoughts after he has stolen a book—without knowing that it is a chess anthology— vividly captures his desperate needs. He hopes that it is an arcane book, which is of very small type, narrowly spaced, and with many letters, so that he can devote all his time and energy to reading it, and eventually to memorising it, if only for the sake of negating the nothingness that envelops him. A chess anthology of one hundred and fifty championship games is all the better, for it provides him with

尚、性格堅毅的優點。王一生過的雖是胼手胝足的日子，可他不以為苦，毫無追名逐利之心，這一點和琴多維奇貪慕錢財與虛榮的性情，恰成鮮明對照。倪斌為了讓王一生參加地區比賽而賄賂地方領導，對此王一生並不領情，而且一口予以拒絕，可見其為人之正直。王一生的內心力量同樣不凡，這一點在漫長的車輪大戰裏尤其表現得淋漓盡致，乙博士顯然難望其項背。在阿城看來，王一生對象棋的忘我熱忱，根本不會危害其心理健康；而且惟有經過以一敵九的磨練，這位略通文墨的棋王方才得以開竅，領悟精神追求的意義，一改以往對精神世界掉以輕心的態度。王一生願意與冠軍言和，更顯出他為人的謙遜與大度。他的作風與琴多維奇的冷傲與乙博士的好勝，實在不可同日而語。在阿城筆下，普通人其實一點兒也不普通。他不僅聰明過人，而且堅定無比；一旦有所領悟，便可面對挑戰，克服困難，並超越自己。

　　兩篇小說的敘述者，起初都把下棋視為遊戲，是身處困境時紓緩壓力與焦慮的一種手段。主人公沉迷象棋，動機也不外逃避令人難堪的現實。乙博士是在被蓋世太保軟禁以後，才開始學習下棋的。被囚的日子空虛難耐，他惟有想盡一切辦法保持心智清醒。小說裏有一段描寫他偷書時的心理活動，極其生動的表現了他的絕望之情。當時他還不知道到手的是棋譜，只希望那是一本深奧難懂、字體極小、排版細密、文字極多的著作，好讓他耗盡心神細讀，然後銘記於心；惟有這樣，他才可以打發那無窮無盡的虛無日子。後來他發現那是一本棋書，彙編了一百五十局冠軍大賽的棋譜，自然

"a weapon against the strangling monotony of space and time". Ironically, chess turns out to be the main cause of his nervous breakdown. First the joy of play becomes a lust for play; then the lust for play becomes a compulsion to play. In the end, the compulsion to play against oneself results in a self-produced schizophrenia, a monomania of "chess poisoning" fuelled by the insatiable desire to win.

Unlike Dr. B, Wang has never faced political persecutions. Yet life is not easy for Wang either. As an orphan, he has to struggle for survival, especially in a time of social unrest and food shortages. His sole solace in life is total immersion in chess, as expressed in his favourite lines, "How may melancholy be dispelled, save through chess?" Without realising it, he is actually driven by an intense need to transcend the daily grind by indulging himself in the intriguing world of chess. This explains in part why he takes unpaid leave from his job and wanders across the countryside for weeks just to look for an opponent. In a sense, he is trying to break away from the unbearable dullness of his life. In this regard, he is very much a spiritual kin of Dr. B.

The one-track obsession and remarkable feats of major characters in both stories are witnessed and recounted by the narrators. Interestingly, both narrators show very little interest in chess. As observers, they seem to be more concerned with the psychological and philosophical implications of the game to the players. For the Austrian narrator in Zweig's novel, chess is just a pastime that kills boredom, sharpens the senses, and exhilarates the spirit, but as a sport it cannot be taken too seriously. In his eyes, it is simply inconceivable, if not downright ridiculous, that any sapient person would be entirely wrapped up in a single idea, or even more preposterously, devoting his mental energy exclusively to the limited space of the checkered board. Any such obsession either exposes the person's intellectual limitations, as in the case of Czentovic, or leads to pathological monomania, as in the case of Dr. B, for there are other occupations

喜出望外。此書成了他的「神奇武器」，用來「抵禦時空所產生的那種令人窒息的死寂」。反諷的是，下棋竟導致他的心智失常。開始學棋的時候，其樂無窮，不覺其害；成了嗜好以後，沉溺其中，便不能自拔。自我對弈使他精神分裂，求勝心更使到這種「象棋中毒」的偏執狂越演越烈。

王一生的處境和乙博士不同，他沒有遭到政治迫害，可是他的生活也不容易。身為孤兒，他必須掙扎求存；在政治動盪、糧食短缺的年代裏，他的日子尤其艱難。他生命裏唯一的安慰就是下棋，用他最喜歡的話來說，就是「何以解憂？唯有象棋」。他並沒有意識到，他之所以沉迷象棋，其實是受到內心要超越日常磨難的強烈欲望所驅使。若非如此，他何苦告長假，出遠門，四處找人下棋？顯然，他想擺脫這種日復一日的刻板生涯。就這一點而言，他和乙博士是有共通之處的。

兩篇小說裏主人公的棋癖和棋藝，一一由冷眼旁觀的敘述者細細道來。有趣的是，兩名敘述者對下棋根本毫無興趣。身為旁觀者，他們似乎更關心這種遊戲對局中人所造成的心理或哲理方面的影響。對於茨威格小說裏的奧地利敘述者而言，下棋只是一種消遣，它可以消磨時間，訓練心智，振奮精神；可是，象棋既然只是一種體育運動，自然不必把它看得太重要。他認為，聰明人不可能光做一件事；若將全副精力放在小小的棋盤上，更是荒唐透頂。單一的嗜好只不過顯示了當事人的局限，琴多維奇便是一例；單一的嗜好也可能使當事人患上偏執狂，就好像乙博士那樣。言下之意，

and values in life that are more imperative and worthy of devotion. In short, the sympathetic narrator of Zweig's novel has a cautious, sceptical and somewhat negative attitude towards chess, even when it has the potential to mitigate existential angst as in the extreme situation of Dr. B.

The narrator in A Cheng's story does not like chess either. This is one of the reasons why he has only tepid interest in Wang at the beginning. But as the story proceeds, the similar hardships that they both have undergone as orphans bring them closer together, irrespective of their obvious differences in class and outlook. As Wang's friend, the narrator is fascinated by Wang's unremitting devotion to chess. It soon becomes apparent to him that Wang's single-minded passion for chess is at least as important to his life as his endeavours to maintain basic subsistence, despite Wang's repeated denial of the significance of chess. As the story draws to a close after Wang's great victory, both Wang and the narrator begin to understand the larger implication of the game of chess. Now they can appreciate its value as a humble means for an ordinary man to achieving a truly meaningful life. While Wang fumbles for words to express his feelings, the narrator has already drawn his own conclusion:

> I smiled and then thought: If I weren't a common person, how could I know such joy? With my family dead and gone and my hair cut short, I shoulder a hoe every day; but this is a truly human life. To comprehend this is happiness and good fortune itself. Food and clothing are the basic things. Ever since mankind existed, they have been kept busy every day for them. But it is not really human to be limited to them.*

---

* In order to follow the meaning of the Chinese text as closely as possible, I have compromised between W.J.F. Jenner's and Michael S. Duke's translations by quoting them eclectically and modifying them slightly where necessary. Duke has translated some of the important passages in his article "Two Chess Masters: One Chinese Way".

即人生還有其他遠比象棋更重要、更值得我們為之獻身的事業與追求。簡而言之，茨威格小說裏的敘述者雖然語帶同情，知道在類似乙博士的極端處境裏，象棋確實有紓緩生存焦慮的作用，可是他對象棋還是抱着謹慎、懷疑，甚至否定的態度。

〈棋王〉的敘述者同樣不喜歡象棋。這也是他最初對王一生不感興趣的一個原因。不過，兩人因為同為孤兒，遭遇相近，所以終能放下階級差異和世界觀的分歧，而成為摯友。敘述者對朋友的嗜好感到好奇，自是意料中事。儘管王一生一再強調為生不為棋的觀點，敘述者卻明白精神慰藉其實對王一生非常重要；象棋既能養性，它在王一生生命裏的地位，不可能在求生本能之下。到了故事的尾聲，王一生大勝四方之後，兩人方才領會象棋的真義。象棋的價值，在於它可以讓一個普通百姓以最簡樸的方式，過上有意義的生活。王一生不擅辭令，未能表達心裏的感受，敘述者卻已有定論：

> 我笑起來，想：不做俗人，哪兒會知道這般樂趣？家破人亡，平了頭每日荷鋤，卻自有真人生在裏面，識到了，即是幸，即是福。衣食是本，自有人類，就是每日在忙這個。可囿在其中，終於還不太像人。

Obviously, chess is now regarded by the narrator as spiritual sustenance rather than a mere pastime. It also begins to outweigh basic subsistence in Wang's mind. In this regard, A Cheng seems more willing to ascribe positive values to the game than Stefan Zweig.

II

For literary critics, "The Chess Master" is a story not just about chess, but also about a way of life. Chess denotes not so much a game that is confined by rules and the material presence of the chess set, as a mental exercise and even spiritual freedom with very strong metaphysical coloration. The relative insignificance of materiality, as represented by the chess set, is adumbrated at the beginning of the story. This is particularly evident in the fact that Wang can always take on any opponent even without the chess set. The chess pieces that he treasures most are those made from toothbrush handles by his mother, without any Chinese inscriptions on them. In other words, they serve no practical purpose except as a keepsake, indicating his fond memories of his mother. In terms of material worth, Wang's primitive chess set undoubtedly pales in comparison with Ni Bin's ebony chess set, which is an antique from the Ming dynasty. Yet this is exactly where the real meaning of the unmarked chess set emerges— a real chess master requires no chess sets; his imagination and ability to calculate are what counts. In short, he has the ability to transcend the materiality that means so much to an ordinary man. Towards the end of the multiple game, Wang seems to have transformed from a good chess player into a supernatural being. His ability to foresee his opponents' moves is described as clairvoyance and wisdom:

> Wang Yisheng was sitting alone in the big room, staring towards us, his
> hands on his knees, a slender pillar of iron who seemed to hear and see

　　至此敘述者顯然不再將象棋視為簡單的遊戲，而是將之奉為養性之道。王一生本人亦開始領悟，養性其實比維生來得重要。就這一點而言，阿城似乎較茨威格更願意賦予象棋正面的意義。

二

　　對於文學評論家來說，〈棋王〉寫的不僅是下棋，而且是生活的方式。象棋，與其說是一種受制於棋具和規則的遊戲，不如說是一種心智的活動，甚或是一種充滿形而上色彩的心靈逍遙遊。故事伊始，就以象棋此一道具暗示有形之物其實並不重要；王一生經常下盲棋，正是這個意思。他所珍惜的無字棋，是母親用牙刷把給他做的，沒有實際的用途，只不過是他感念母恩的紀念物。這一套粗糙的棋具，自然沒有倪斌的烏木象棋那麼值錢，那可是明代的古董。然而，這正是無字棋的真義所在：真正的大師手中無棋，心中有棋；想像力與預見能力才是象棋的關鍵所在。一言以蔽之，普通人所關切的有形之物，大師一無掛礙。到了車輪大戰的尾聲，王一生彷彿已經擺脫棋手的凡身，羽化成仙；他推敲棋路的本領，儼然成了看透紅塵的智慧：

　　王一生孤身一人坐在大屋子中央，瞪眼看着我們，雙手支在膝上，鐵鑄一個細樹樁，似無所見，似無所聞。高高的一盞電

nothing. A single lamp high above him shone dimly on his face. His eyes were sunken, and very dark. It was as if they were looking down at the vast and boundless universe. All his life force seemed to be concentrated in his mop of tousled hair. For a long time it did not disperse, then it gradually spread out, burning our faces.

To understand the significance accorded to the game and A Cheng's positive portrayal of the chess player, a short detour into the context in which the story was written is in order. The story of "The Chess Master" was conceived in the early 1980s, when China was in the throes of a profound cultural crisis. Following the death of Mao Zedong in 1976 and the subsequent palace coup that brought down the "Gang of Four", an era of ultraleftism and xenophobia in China came to an end. A pragmatic Chinese government soon denounced "The Great Proletarian Cultural Revolution" (1966–1976), sounded the clarion call for the "Four Modernisations", and opened up China to the rest of the world. In the frenzied years that followed, Chinese writers and scholars began to enjoy a modicum of freedom of speech, though from time to time it was overshadowed by political campaigns triggered by intra-party factional strife. Across the country, literary salons and journals of various persuasions mushroomed; seminars and conferences in different fields were organised. However, in the midst of the so-called "post-1976 euphoria", an acute sense of cultural crisis began to surge in the intellectual circles. Faced with the appalling devastation caused by the Cultural Revolution, the general disillusionment with Communist utopianism, and the rapid pace of modernisation, the disorientated Chinese intellectuals felt an urgent need to revisit the past, salvage cultural traditions and refashion a new cultural identity for themselves and the nation. Their intense interest in cultural issues and grave concern for the future of China eventually led to a large-scale intellectual movement known as the "Cultural Craze".

燈，暗暗地照在他臉上，眼睛深陷進去，黑黑的似俯視大千世界，茫茫宇宙。那生命像聚在一頭亂髮中，久久不散，又慢慢彌漫開來，灼得人臉熱。

　　要理解阿城筆下象棋的涵義以及王一生的正面形象，有必要檢視小說的寫作背景。〈棋王〉創作於八十年代初，當時的中國大陸正面臨一場嚴峻的文化危機。1976年，隨着毛澤東的逝世以及「四人幫」的鋃鐺下獄，極左與鎖國的時代乃一去不復返。務實的領導班子旋即否定「無產階級文化大革命」（1966–1976），推行「四個現代化」，並實行開放政策。接下來的日子熱火朝天，作家與學者雖然仍不時受到黨內鬥爭所引發的政治運動所干擾，但已經有了初步的言論自由。在全國範圍內，文藝沙龍與形形色色的雜誌如雨後春筍般湧現，各類的講座與學術會議也競相舉辦。可是，在新時期的歡樂氣氛裏，知識界開始意識到文化的危機。文革的浩劫，共產主義信仰的破產，和急速的現代化進程，使中國的知識分子若有所失，並感到有重新認識歷史，挽救文化傳統，為自己以及國人建立新文化身份的必要。他們對傳統文化和中國未來的關心，促成了聲勢浩大的「文化熱」思潮。

The literary circle responded in December 1984, when a forum for young writers and critics was held in Hangzhou. The forum initiated the "Search for Roots" movement of 1985–1986. After the meeting, Han Shaogong, a novelist from the South, published the seminal article "Roots of Literature" in 1985. He appealed to Chinese men of letters to carry out an in-depth cultural reflection, and encouraged them to represent the core of Chinese culture in their literary writings. For him, a literature not steeped in history and culture represented a literature without soul and identity. Han's article sparked enthusiastic responses. In a few months, the whirlwind to "search for roots" swept through the Chinese literary scene. A Cheng, Li Hangyu, Zheng Wanlong and some other writers took part in the discussion.

If Han was considered a vanguard from the South, A Cheng was hailed as a representative of the North. "The Chess Master", published a year before Han's programmatic article went to press, was applauded by critics as a precursor of the movement as well as a major contribution to its success. A Cheng shared much of his peers' concern about their lack of formal education and inadequate understanding of traditional Chinese culture. He also believed that a deep understanding of culture is the prerequisite of a good piece of literature. Like other young writers taking part in the movement, he was convinced that the great formal tradition of elite culture had already been lost on the Chinese mainland, what had survived was merely conventions or informal culture, precariously preserved by the common folks in the remote areas untouched by the process of modernisation and political campaigns. In a recent dialogue with a calligrapher, A Cheng even bluntly suggested that Chinese calligraphy as an art and culture no longer exists; what remains today is nothing but the bald technique of writing Chinese characters with a brush. However, sceptical as he is about the survival of a great cultural tradition, A Cheng has tried to steer away from cynicism and pessimism in his works of fiction. As a matter of

　　1984年12月，在杭州舉辦的一個年輕作家與評論家的座談會上，文學界作出了回應。座談會催生了1985年至1986年間的「尋根」運動。座談會結束之後，南方的小說家韓少功在1985年發表了一篇重要文章：〈文學的根〉。他呼籲作家作深刻的文化反思，並鼓勵大家在作品裏表現中華文化的神髓。對他來說，沒有歷史傳統與文化氣脈的文學作品，是既缺乏生氣也沒有民族自我的平庸之作。韓少功的文章引起熱烈的反響，不出數月，「尋根」之風席捲大陸文壇。阿城、李杭育、鄭萬隆等作家也參與了討論。

　　如果韓少功是南方的急先鋒，阿城就是北方的代表人物。〈棋王〉較韓少功的綱領文章早一年發表，被論者認為是文學尋根運動的先聲，也是是次運動的主要成就。阿城與許多同代作家一樣，因為無緣接受正規的教育，對傳統文化的認識不深，而耿耿於懷。他認同韓少功的説法，深信對文化的深入了解，是好作品的先決條件。他和不少參加尋根運動的年輕作家的看法一樣，認為中華文化的大傳統已經從中國大陸消失，剩下的惟有民間的小傳統而已。而民間的習俗，也只有在遠離政治運動、尚未現代化的邊遠地區，方得以零星保存。有一次，阿城和書法家對談，他甚至唐突直言，謂傳統的書法藝術與文化其實早已失傳，民間所存徒有寫毛筆字的技巧而已。儘管阿城不相信文化傳承的可能，他的小説卻絲毫不沾犬儒悲

fact, his emotive attachment to the informal aspects of culture and their material manifestations are so strong that many such passages in his fiction radiate ardour and joy. His empathy with the common folks also endows him with the perspicacity to reveal what is unusual about the most nondescript characters.

A Cheng's cultural populism explains in part why in "The Chess Master", the secrets of the "way of chess" are kept in the hands of an ordinary old man and the *homo obscurissimus* is the real chess master. A Cheng seems to be saying that the fate of the residue of the Chinese cultural tradition is in the hands of common men such as Wang Yisheng. The mysterious "way of chess" and the peculiar image of Wang Yisheng have given rise to many interpretations. Michael S. Duke, for instance, holds that chess in this story represents the primacy of spiritual sustenance in a truly human life. For him, such sustenance comes from the cherished values of traditional Chinese culture, as symbolised by chess and the "way of chess" passed down from the wise old man to Wang. Wang's final victory affirms not only the necessity of abstract values in general, but also the imperative of transmitting the true spiritual heritage of traditional China in particular. Such an implicit message of salvaging a national tradition becomes all the more significant if the reader takes the backdrop of the story into consideration. The story takes place precisely in the midst of the Cultural Revolution—a time of rampant iconoclasm and relentless anti-traditionalism, when old-fashioned scholars were brutalised, suspicious books burnt and cultural relics destroyed.

Kam Louie's remarks on chess, or the "way of chess", chime with the general view that it is an abstraction of the Chinese cultural tradition, or "Chineseness". But he also points out the vagueness of such a notion, for "there are no explicit portrayals of the specific traditional morality that would be salvaged". According to him, the only strain of Chinese philosophical tradition appropriated by A Cheng

觀的氣息。事實上，阿城對民間習俗與器物情有獨鍾，筆墨所及之處無不神采飛揚。他與老百姓休戚與共，對他們觀察入微，故此他的小說以表現平凡人物的不凡之處見長。

這種文化上的民粹立場，解釋了為什麼在〈棋王〉裏，中華棋道的奧秘掌握在無名老者的手裏，而真正的棋王竟是一個貌不驚人的無名小卒。阿城的言下之意，莫非殘餘的中華文化，正掌握在王一生這類小人物的手裏？玄之又玄的「棋道」，形象獨特的王一生，的確引起讀者諸多的闡釋。比方說，杜邁可便認為，小說裏的象棋意味着人的精神境界；一個沒有精神世界的人，終究不太像人。對杜邁可來說，精神世界由傳統文化所珍惜的道德價值所構成，在小說裏以象棋和棋道作為象徵，通過智慧老人而得以傳授給王一生。王一生最後的大捷，不僅確認了抽象價值的重要，也宣示了將傳統文化傳授給年輕一代的必要。若考慮到小說所描寫的故事背景，此一保存民族文化傳統的信息就顯得格外的寓意深長。〈棋王〉的故事發生於文革時期，正是打倒傳統和否定一切的年代；焚書坑儒，毀壞文物的事件，簡直無日無之。

雷金慶對象棋或棋道的解讀和一般的看法相同，他認為象棋所指的是中華文化或「中華特性」。可是，他也批評此說的含混之處，因為小說「究竟要挽救何種傳統美德，實在語焉不詳」。根據他的看法，阿城在小說裏採用的只有道家的觀念，特別是老子的樸素說

in the story is Daoism—the Daoism of the rustic Laozi in particular. The two old men, especially the garbage collector, are but modern images of the traditional Daoist hermit. The garbage collector's arcane exposition on the "way of chess"—and especially the part on the tactics of "softness"—certainly resonates with the passages of *Daode Jing: The Book of the Way*. While Michael S. Duke sees in Wang's immersion in chess an indication of his spiritual and moral autonomy, Louie detects in it the motif of escapism inherent in Daoism. Apart from the two old men who choose to live in obscurity, Wang is another example of a humble genius bent on mental and spiritual escape. Wang cares very little about what happens around him, political or otherwise, except for his basic subsistence. In Louie's view, Wang's unusual behaviour unmistakably appears as Daoist passiveness and escapism.

What Louie sees in Wang as an unwillingness to take affirmative social action is interpreted by Theodore Huters as a backhanded act of defiance. By invoking a non-orthodox tradition of Chinese thought, which is rustic Daoism, A Cheng makes chess not so much an ideal refuge from as a strong challenge to the daily politics of the Chinese state. The metaphysical aura of chess, as invoked in the final scene depicting Wang's trance-like conditions, further enhances the game's transcendent value as a counterpoint to the dreary and dreadful political environment. To some extent, one may even say that Wang's, as well as the narrator's, aversion to the political events, is analogous to A Cheng's conspicuous reticence over the atrocities of the Cultural Revolution in his works. Obviously the narrator in "The Chess Master" would rather focus on the most common chess game among the Chinese that can normally bring people together, than zero in on the violent death of his parents in political persecution. To borrow a phrase from Leo Ou-fan Lee, A Cheng's focus on cultural activities rather than political events is a form of anti-political politics. Writing in the 1980s, A Cheng was in tune with his times. It was a time when culture

法。小說裏的兩位老者，其實都是返樸歸真的現代隱士。拾荒老者
尤具古風，他對棋道的解釋，玄之又玄；處弱守柔之說，更與《道德
經》遙相呼應。如果杜邁可認為王一生的嗜好表現了人的尊嚴與自
主，雷金慶則從中嗅到道家遁世的氣味。除了兩名遺世獨立的老者
以外，王一生也是一名向心靈深處尋求慰藉的無名奇才。王一生只
求溫飽，對世事漠不關心；在雷金慶看來，這種獨特的行徑完全是
道家消極無為的表現。

　　雷金慶眼中的消極行為，在胡志德看來卻是一種低調的抵抗：
阿城通過非主流的道家思想傳統，賦予象棋活動一種無為的精神，
用來挑戰無所不為、無孔不入的國家政治；象棋已經不僅僅是理想
的避難所而已。在小說的最後一幕裏，王一生近似入定的精神狀
態，更使象棋充滿了形而上的氣氛。這種寫法凸顯了象棋的價值，
正在其超越世俗的可能；象棋，是令人厭煩與恐懼的政治環境的對
立面。在某個程度上，王一生和敘述者迴避政治，和阿城不願在小
說裏描寫文革慘事的道理相同。〈棋王〉的敘述者大談老少皆宜的象
棋，而不提雙親被迫害致死的事件，顯然是一種張揚文化、貶抑政
治的春秋筆法。套用李歐梵的話，這是一種反政治的政治策略。阿
城的創作與時代同呼吸，共命運；在八十年代，藝術家和作家要抗

was called upon by artists and writers to relieve the oppressive omnipresence of politics.

For his part, Huters argues that since too much emphasis has been laid upon chess as a bearer of traditional Chinese culture, the story goes awry in the latter part and suffers from the reification of a cultural motif. The openness of the first two sections of the story, as evidenced in the narrator and Wang's comradeship as well as Ni and Wang's mutual respect despite their differences and disagreements, gradually gives way to the discordant ending that upholds the "way of chess", or certain values of the cultural tradition, as the absolute value in life. The possibility of pluralism is thus denied. In this regard, A Cheng is no less a neo-traditionalist than his predecessors of the early twentieth century, who were equally obsessed with the idea of "National Essence". In Huters's opinion, such an obsession with and reification of culture only come into existence at a time of grave cultural crisis, when the intellectuals begin to sense the disintegration of the world around them and strive to hold fast to values in however vestigial a form.

The writers involved in the "Search for Roots" movement definitely sensed the urgency of rectifying the situation. Their various approaches to salvage culture from the ruins of politics can be regarded as the collective effort of a ravaged generation in a desperate attempt to hold on to a meaningful life and refashion a respectable cultural identity for themselves and the nation. Wang Yisheng may be too naive to understand the importance of his spiritual needs, but the sophisticated narrator knows better. Towards the end of the story, he summarises succinctly for Wang, for himself, and perhaps as the commentators would argue, for the disillusioned nation as well. Without the traditional "way of chess", what would Wang Yisheng be but a life (*yisheng*) wasted (*wang*) ?

衡無所不在、令人喘不過氣的政治，靠的正是文化。

對於胡志德而言，由於小説過分強調象棋的文化象徵意義，使到小説的後半部出現問題，而且有把文化母題僵化之嫌。小説的前兩節，不論敘述者和王一生，還是王一生和倪斌，都有存異求同的氣量，因此小説呈現出一種開放的狀態；可是到了末尾，由於小説高舉「棋道」或中華之道，作為一種至高無上的價值，小説便顯得很不協調，文化多元的可能性也因此遭到扼殺。就這一點而言，阿城較諸二十世紀初期心繫國粹的前輩，實在不遑多讓，算得上是一位新派的傳統文化捍衛者。據胡志德的看法，這種對文化的執迷以及將之物化的現象，只有在文化出現嚴重危機的時候才會浮現。知識分子一旦意識到身邊的世界開始分崩離析，他們會為了維護殘存的價值觀念而力挽狂瀾。

「尋根」運動的作家肯定意識到形勢之嚴峻，才各施各法，祈望將文化從政治的廢墟裏搶救出來。他們的不同主張，見證的是正是飽歷滄桑的一代，為了保存生命的意義，為了替知識分子和中華民族重塑有尊嚴的文化身份，所作的無望努力。王一生為人簡單，未能掌握精神文明的真諦；思想複雜的敘述者，對此卻瞭然於胸。故事完結之前，他所説的那一段話，替王一生和他自己作了言簡意賅的總結；評論者或許還會補充，這一段話也是為了幻想破滅的中華民族而發的。如果傳統的「棋道」不存，王一生只會枉過一生，終究也不太像人。

III

A Cheng has been widely lauded by literary critics and general readers alike as a skilful storyteller. In fact, his talent for storytelling was first discovered by the students and peasants at the national farm where he worked, long before he became a writer. According to an anecdote recounted by Bonnie S. McDougall, the students and peasants were so enthralled by his tales that they were willing to offer him meat and cigarettes, which were in quite short supply at that time, in exchange for his stories. Eventually A Cheng became so popular that he could, in McDougall's words, "pick his own audience according to who offered the best meal". He would recount stories that he had read in school, and modify some of the foreign stories to comply with Chinese customs and morality for his audience. When the British television version of *Anna Karenina* was broadcast in China in 1984, some of the peasant audience were angry with A Cheng, for they thought they had been deceived by him with his own adaptation. In other words, they accused A Cheng of deviating from the original version.

There was once an original version of "The Chess Master", which seemed to have existed only in A Cheng's oral performance. As Li Tuo fondly recalled in the early 1990s, it was one winter evening in 1983 when several writers, including A Cheng, were invited to dinner at his apartment. During the meal, someone tempted A Cheng to entertain the guests with a story. A Cheng agreed but did not begin until he was replete. The tale he recounted that evening was so captivating that the audience urged him to put it into writing afterwards. That was purportedly the germ of "The Chess Master". Although the published version is different from—and according to Li, less exciting than—the original one, it was an instant success. Right after its publication in Shanghai, the story won two literary awards, the Award for

三

阿城的說書技巧，為批評家與讀者推崇備至。事實上，早在成名之前，還在農村插隊的時候，阿城已經以會講故事出名了。據杜博妮所說，知青和農民都非常喜歡聽阿城講故事，所以他們願意以當時非常稀罕的肉和煙來犒勞阿城，以換取一段故事。阿城後來名氣很大，可以挑選聽眾。照杜博妮的說法，就是唯伙食佳者得聽故事。阿城的段子源自學校裏讀來的故事，外國故事則略加修改，以符國情。1984年，英國的電視劇《安娜‧卡列尼娜》在中國播出的時候，有些聽過阿城說故事的農民大表不滿，因為他們覺得阿城改編了故事，把他們給騙了。換句話說，他們覺得阿城不應擅改原著。

〈棋王〉原來另有版本，就是阿城的口頭演出。根據李陀在九十年代初的深情回憶，1983年的一個冬夜，他請了作家朋友到家裏聚餐，阿城亦是座上客。吃飯的時候，有人慫恿阿城來一段故事，娛樂大家。阿城沒反對，可是要等到吃飽喝足了才願意開腔。當晚他講的故事太精彩，事後大家都催促他把故事寫下來。按李陀的說法，此即小說〈棋王〉之源起。儘管後來的小說與原來的講述有別，而且——依李陀之見——也沒有原來的故事那麼扣人心弦，可小說還是一鳴驚人，在上海甫出版，立刻贏得兩個文學獎：福建《中篇

Distinguished Literary Works, given by the *Journal of Selected Novellas* of Fujian Province in 1984, and the National Award for Distinguished Novellas of 1983–1984. The enthusiasm was soon repeated overseas. When the story was published in a Hong Kong journal in September 1985, a month after Michael S. Duke's enthusiastic review had appeared, A Cheng began to draw a large readership outside the mainland. Following the story's publication in Taiwan, A Cheng became so popular that an "A Cheng Fever", as some commentators would call it, ensued. The success of the story also attracted the attention of the film industry. Two directors, Teng Wenji from the mainland, and Yim Ho from Hong Kong, adapted the story into films in 1988 and 1991, bearing the titles *Chess King* and *King of Chess* respectively.* A Cheng's popularity among Chinese readers has not declined with the passage of time. According to a poll conducted in 1999 by the Editorial Department of *Asiaweek* and fourteen prominent Chinese literary critics, "The Chess Master" made it to the list of The Best One Hundred Chinese Fictions of the Twentieth Century. In short, it has become one of the classics of modern Chinese literature.

A Cheng's next two acclaimed stories, "The Tree Master" and "The Children's Master", were published in 1985. "The Tree Master" is a story about the clash of beliefs between sent-down students and local peasants. Set during the peak of the Cultural Revolution in southwestern China, a group of urban students, led by Li Li, a devout Maoist, is on a mission to rebuild China by clearing a forest for farmland. No peasants dare to stand in their way until the students' intention to chop down a giant tree in the forest, regarded by the native

---

* Yim Ho combined A Cheng's story with Chang Hsi-kuo's novel of the same title into *King of Chess*. Chang's novel was published in Taiwan in 1975. However, Yim did not complete the film. Tsui Hark took over the direction later.

小説選刊》的1984年優秀作品獎和第三屆全國優秀中篇小説獎。海外的反應同樣熱烈。1985年9月，香港的一份雜誌在發表杜邁可熱情洋溢的評論之後的一個月，全文刊登〈棋王〉，旋即吸引不少海外讀者。小説在台灣出版之後，論者所説的「阿城熱」已然形成。小説風靡一時，亦引起了電影業的興趣。大陸導演滕文驥和香港導演嚴浩，分別在1988年和1991年，將小説改編為兩部同名電影。*阿城受讀者歡迎的程度，並不曾隨時間的過去而稍減。1999年，《亞洲周刊》編輯部和十四位著名文學批評家投票挑選一百部二十世紀最佳中文小説，〈棋王〉榮登金榜。〈棋王〉已成現代文學的經典。

　　阿城另外兩篇膾炙人口的小説是〈樹王〉和〈孩子王〉，發表於1985年。〈樹王〉講述的是知青與農民之間的信仰衝突。故事發生在文革的高潮，一群下放到西南地區的知青，為了改天換地的墾殖大業而砍伐山林，為首的是高舉毛澤東思想紅旗的李立。他們的革命大業，農民豈敢過問？可是當他們要砍下一棵當地人視為神樹的參天古木的時候，農民的態度就變了。大部分的人消極抵抗，只有蕭

---

* 嚴浩將阿城的小説與張系國的同名長篇小説融為一體，改編為電影。嚴浩並沒有完成拍攝工作，後來由徐克接手完成。

population as the sacred King of Trees, is revealed. While most peasants refuse to cooperate, only one man, nicknamed Knotty Xiao, stands up to the students to protect the tree. Although the dramatic confrontation ends with Knotty Xiao's failure, the scene points out the peasants' respect for nature and naive sense of ecological conservation, which resonate with traditional Chinese wisdom. Knotty Xiao's attempt to conserve a single tree is not only a critique of the students' blind faith in the political slogan of "Man can conquer Heaven", but also an indication of the losing battle waged by the residual conscience of a culture against the massive destruction carried out in the name of the Cultural Revolution.

"The Children's Master" is another tale of a man who swims against the tide of the Cultural Revolution. Lao Gar, a student with high school education, is transferred from a state farm to a primary school in a nearby village to take up a teaching position. Appalled by the wretchedness of the school and the pupils' ignorance, he decides to teach the deprived children something useful. He deviates from official syllabuses that promote not so much knowledge as ideology, and comes up with some practical measures of his own to help his students learn more efficiently. Under his guidance, the students, especially Wang Fu, the most diligent among them, begin to make great strides in learning. However, Lao Gar's unorthodox teaching does not last long. When local authorities learn of his offbeat pedagogy, he is fired. Before he departs, Lao Gar leaves a dictionary—which is the only dictionary available in that remote area—to Wang Fu as a parting gift. The dictionary symbolises not only traditional respect for learning, but also a hope for the transmission of culture.

Inspired by the story, the Chinese director Chen Kaige adapted "The Children's Master" and made it into a film called "King of the Children" in 1987. Although Chen once laboured alongside A Cheng and shared much of his experiences in southwestern China, his attitude

疙瘩一人挺身而出，捍衛樹王。雖然蕭疙瘩的反抗以失敗告終，可是這戲劇性的一幕，卻展現了農民對自然的敬畏和純樸的環保意識，他們的立場和傳統的智慧是一脈相承的。蕭疙瘩捨命護樹，無疑是對知青迷信「人定勝天」的政治口號的當頭棒喝，可是也顯示了在以「文化革命」為名的大毀滅面前，僅存的文化良知竟是如此的無能為力。

〈孩子王〉也是一個關於逆文革潮流而行的人物的故事。有高中教育程度的知青老桿兒，從農場調到鄰村的小學當教師。學校的簡陋，學生的無知，叫老桿兒大吃一驚。他決心把書教好，讓窮孩子學些有用的東西。由於教材充斥着政治八股，對學生毫無用處，他只好棄之不用，自行授課。他教導有方，學生果然進步不小，用功的王福更是成績斐然。可惜好景不長，地方領導了解到他那離經叛道的教學方法之後，便把他給撤了。老桿兒離職之前，把山區裏唯一的一本字典送給王福留念。這本字典所象徵的，不僅是傳統中國人對學問的敬重，也是對文化傳承的一點希望。

大陸導演陳凱歌受到〈孩子王〉的啟發，於1987年將之改編為同名電影。陳凱歌曾經和阿城同在西南地區勞動，兩人的插隊經歷非

towards education and tradition, as presented in the film, is drastically different from, if not altogether contradicting, A Cheng's. Nevertheless, the impressive cinematography, complex nuance and radical iconoclasm of the film make it another tour de force of Chen. In the film expert Tony Rayns's opinion, it is as definitive a film as A Cheng's story is in its reflection on the trials and rewards of the sent-down students' experience in the Chinese backlands. It is a fair guess that the film will be equally remembered in years to come as one of the classics of the New Chinese Cinema.

Like many of his contemporaries, A Cheng is an autodidact. Born in 1949 into a cultured family, he could have benefited from family education and formal schooling had it not for the outbreaks of the Anti-Rightist Campaign in 1957 and the Cultural Revolution in 1966. His father, Zhong Dianfei, a major film critic who was in charge of the film section of the Communist Party's Propaganda Bureau, was suspended from his job in 1957 for his open criticism of the Party's political interference in the film industry. After a spell of "reform through labour" in the countryside, Zhong resumed his position in the early 1960s, only to be deposed again in 1966, when the Cultural Revolution broke out. Zhong's political downfall not only disrupted the family's normal life, but also consequentially barred A Cheng from receiving university education. Since all schools closed down during the Cultural Revolution, A Cheng decided to go to the countryside and work in a state farm in 1968, following the footsteps of millions of city high school students. He then stayed in Shanxi, Inner Mongolia and Yunnan for over a decade and moved back to Beijing in 1979, when the Cultural Revolution was over and life resumed its normal course.

A Cheng was a painter before turning to literature. According to Bonnie S. McDougall, A Cheng had loved drawing since childhood. That he had chosen to work in those remote areas of China has much

常相似，可是陳凱歌透過電影所表達的對傳統與教育的態度，卻和
阿城的原作迥然有別，甚至南轅北轍。不過，此片的攝影動人，意
蘊複雜，反傳統的意識強烈，是陳凱歌的又一力作。依電影專家湯
尼‧雷恩之見，此片對知青上山下鄉的得失有深刻的反思，與阿城
的小說難分高下。此片日後成為當代大陸新電影的經典之作，應不
難想見。

　　阿城和許多同代人一樣，都是靠自學成才的。1949年，他出生
於一個文人家庭。如果不是受到1957年的反右運動和1966年的文化
大革命的衝擊，他本來有機會得到家庭的薰陶和正規的學校教育。
他的父親鍾惦棐是重要的影評人，本來掌管中共宣傳部電影小組的
工作，1957年因公開批評共產黨對電影事業的干預而被拉下馬。他
經過一段時間的「勞動改造」之後，在六十年代初期重返工作崗位。
1966年文革爆發，他再次丟官。鍾惦棐政治上的失勢，不僅影響一
家人的正常生活，還斷送了阿城日後報考大學的機會。文革時期，
學校紛紛停課。1968年，成千上萬的城市學生上山下鄉，阿城也決
定到農村去。他一去十年，到過山西、內蒙和雲南插隊。文革結束
後，生活恢復正常，阿城在1979年回到北京。

　　阿城從事文學創作之前，是個畫家。杜博妮說，阿城從小就愛

to do with his fantasy that these places might offer him more luxuriant subjects for painting. When A Cheng returned to Beijing in 1979, he was invited to take part in an art exhibition organised by Huang Rui and Ma Desheng. Wang Keping, Qu Leilei, Yan Li, Bo Yun, Li Shuang, Mao Lizi, Yang Yiping and many other artists joined them later on. Frustrated by the authorities' refusal to loan them exhibition space, they hung their paintings and sculptures on the railings outside the China Art Gallery in Beijing on 28 September 1979. The exhibition attracted a large crowd. Police interfered, and the street exhibition was cancelled two days later. To press for artistic freedom, the artists then held a public demonstration on the first of October, the National Day of the People's Republic. This daring coterie of non-registered amateur artists has now become very well known in the art history of modern China. They are none other than the Stars, the trailblazers of public exhibition of experimental art in post-Mao China. In August 1980, the Stars were at last given the imprimatur by the authorities to hold their second exhibition in the China Art Gallery. The Stars artists began to leave China in the wake of the exhibitions. Ai Weiwei left in 1981. Li Shuang, who was arrested and sent to a labour camp for her love affair with the French Diplomat Emmanuel Bellefroid, left China in 1983. Wang Keping, Ma Desheng, Yan Li and Qu Leilei soon followed suit. After publishing the three "Master" stories, A Cheng departed for the U.S.A. in 1986. Besides painting and calligraphy, A Cheng is also well-versed in photography. He exhibited a selection of his photographs in a show entitled "Nature, Society and Man" in the 1980s.

In the 1990s, A Cheng followed up his earlier success with four books: *Venice Diary, Confabulations, Common Sense and General Knowledge* and *Winds and Currents Everywhere. Venice Diary* is a collection of his essays, written during his sojourn in Venice, sparingly interspersed with his sketches of Venice. *Confabulations* is a compilation of his public lectures, delivered between 1987 and 1993, on Chinese society and

畫畫；他選擇到邊疆插隊，完全是出於一廂情願的幻想，以為這些地方的題材特別豐富。1979年回到北京後，他應邀參加由黃銳和馬德升發起的藝術展。王克平、曲磊磊、嚴力、薄雲、李爽、毛栗子、楊益平等人稍後加入。由於沒有展覽場地可借，9月28日，他們將參展的畫作和雕塑，統統掛到中國美術館東牆的鐵柵欄上，作露天展出。展覽吸引了很多觀眾，也招來公安的干涉。兩天之後，展覽被迫取消。為了藝術自由，他們在10月1日的國慶日舉行示威遊行。這批一往無前、沒有註冊的業餘藝術家，現已成為中國現代藝術史上一個耀眼的名字：星星。他們是後毛澤東時代，中國實驗藝術展覽的先驅。1980年，星星藝術家終於得到管理當局的批准，在中國美術館舉辦第二次展覽。展覽過後，參展成員紛紛出國，眾星盡散。1981年，艾未未去國。1983年，因與法國外交官白天祥戀愛而被送進勞改營的李爽也離開了中國。隨後，王克平、馬德升、嚴力和曲磊磊相繼投奔異國。阿城在發表「三王」故事之後，也在1986年赴美。除了繪畫和書法，阿城對攝影也頗有心得，八十年代他曾在一個名為「自然，社會，人」的攝影展裏展出作品。

　　九十年代，阿城趁熱打鐵，推出四本作品：《威尼斯日記》、《閒話閒說》、《常識與通識》、《遍地風流》。《威尼斯日記》是他在威尼斯小住時所寫的散文，配有幾幅他親繪的插圖。《閒話閒說》收錄他在1987年到1993年間的演講稿，談的是中國的社會與小說。此書頗為

fiction. This is a small book of wit and sporadic insights, a testimony to A Cheng's good grasp of the informal aspects of Chinese culture. The volume *Common Sense and General Knowledge* includes his articles written for a Chinese periodical between 1997 and 1998. Its variegated subjects range from olfactory sense, ghosts, and soccer to emotional intelligence. *Winds and Currents Everywhere* is the latest collection of his short stories, though most of them were written before his rise to fame. This collection resembles a traditional anecdotage such as *A New Account of Tales of the World* (430 CE) in many ways. As the title suggests, it is a book about the "winds and currents" of contemporary China. The phrase "winds and currents" is an oblique reference to the "winds and currents of Wei and Jin", meaning the spirit of the Wei-Jin Period (220–420). Whereas *A New Account of Tales of the World* captures the zeitgeist of the intellectual elite of the third century by portraying and evaluating individual persons, A Cheng's *Winds and Currents Everywhere* aims at encapsulating the uncommonness of the common people in short stories without passing judgement on them. Although this collection inherits the brevity and seeming casualness of Chinese note-form fiction, it bears the unmistakable stylistic mark of A Cheng's verve and vividness. "Canyon" and "Rope Crossing", two of the best pieces of this collection, give the reader a flavour of the exotic life in southwestern China. "Wet Dreams" is a rare piece of work in A Cheng's corpus that confronts the gory aspect of the Cultural Revolution. Such a harrowing tale of puppy love gone wrong presents a brisk and brutal depiction of the horror and senselessness of political fanaticism. "Making Noodles" is another gem about cherished personal relations, suppressed but unaltered by political persecutions. "Remembrance" is an enjoyably devastating satire of how a naive soldier's loyalty to Chairman Mao gets him into trouble without his ever realising it. The descriptive acumen and insights of these stories once again attest to A Cheng's talent as a storyteller.

精警，時有洞見，足見作者對中國民間文化的了解。《常識與通識》是他在1997年與1998年間為雜誌專欄撰寫的雜文結集，內容涉及嗅覺、鬼狐、足球、情商等題材，無所不談。《遍地風流》是他最新的短篇小說集，蒐羅的幾乎都是他成名之前的作品。這本小說集讀來頗像《世說新語》一類的傳統軼聞集。一如書名所示，本書載述的是當代風流；而「風流」一詞令人想起魏晉風流。如果《世說新語》旨在品題漢末以至於東晉年間名流的言行軼事，為讀者呈現出一個時代的人文風尚，阿城作《遍地風流》，則完全無心月旦人物，只意在凸顯普通老百姓的諸種不凡之處。這本小說集繼承了傳統筆記小說的簡當與樸實，不過阿城小說所獨具的生動氣韻卻一點兒也不少。〈峽谷〉和〈溜索〉為讀者呈現出西南地區的異域風情，是難得的佳作。〈春夢〉直面文革淋漓的鮮血，當屬阿城作品中的異數。少年懷春，轉眼即成噩夢——一個本來催人淚下的故事，由阿城道來竟是如此的果斷與不留餘地，政治狂熱的恐怖與無知實在令人駭然顫抖。〈抻麵〉亦為力作。小說描寫傳統的人情，如何在政治迫害的困境之中，依然藕斷絲連。〈回憶〉裏那名天真的解放軍戰士，因為忠於毛主席而惹來一身麻煩，自己卻懵然不知。這樣的故事令人哭笑不得，足見阿城冷嘲之辛辣。以上諸篇小說，對人情世態體察入微，又一次見證了阿城講故事的天賦。

A Cheng's artistic versatility has also been recognised by the Chinese film industry. Since the 1980s, he has been cooperating with directors such as Xie Jin and Stanley Kwan by writing scripts for them. In the 1990s, he served as art advisor to Hou Hsiao-hsien in his production of *Flowers of Shanghai* (1998). His most recent participation in Chinese film production includes *Springtime in a Small Town* (2002) and *Delamu* (2004), both directed by Tian Zhuangzhuang. A Cheng wrote the script for the film *Springtime in a Small Town*, which is a crafted remake of Fei Mu's classic, *Spring in a Small Town* (1948). *Delamu* is a documentary about the life of travelling merchants, or horse gangs, along a remote and treacherous mountain road, known as the Tea and Horse Road, in southwestern China. A Cheng, who had spent many years living and working in this area, served on Tian's panel of advisors in its production. Recent reports in the Chinese news disclose that Tian Zhuangzhuang has joined hands with A Cheng again. This time Tian will be shooting a film about the life of Wu Qingyuan, a world champion of the game *go* now residing in Japan. A Cheng was assigned the challenging task of preparing the screenplay, based on Wu's autobiography. Whether A Cheng can outperform himself in spinning another rattling good yarn of chess remains to be seen. Yet one thing is for sure: A Cheng's readers definitely would not want to miss this much-anticipated film for the world.

　　阿城多才多藝，早為華語電影界所賞識。從八十年代開始，他已經與謝晉、關錦鵬等導演合作，為他們撰寫劇本。進入九十年代，侯孝賢籌拍《海上花》(1998)，他曾擔當美工顧問。最近幾年，他參與兩部田壯壯的電影製作：《小城之春》(2002) 和《德拉姆》(2004)。阿城為《小城之春》寫劇本，將費穆1948年的同名經典重新搬上銀幕。《德拉姆》是紀錄片，記述中國西南地區的馬幫在茶馬古道上的生涯。阿城曾在此地工作與生活多年，當影片的顧問自然不成問題。據晚近的華文新聞報導，田壯壯與阿城再次攜手合作，新拍的片子以吳清源的生平事迹為題材。吳清源是圍棋大師，曾多次獲得世界冠軍，目前定居日本。阿城的任務是將吳清源的自傳改編為電影劇本，可謂充滿挑戰性。阿城能否超越自己，為讀者和觀眾編織另一個扣人心弦的棋道故事，尚須拭目以待。然而，有一點卻是可以肯定的：阿城的讀者，肯定不會輕易錯過這一部令人充滿期待的電影。

Suggestions for Further Reading

Chow, Rey. "Male Narcissism and National Culture: Subjectivity in Chen Kaige's *King of the Children*". *Primitive Passions: Visuality, Sexuality, Ethnography, and Contemporary Chinese Cinema*. New York: Columbia University Press, 1995. 108–141.

Duke, Michael S. "Two Chess Masters: One Chinese Way: A Comparison of Chang Hsi-kuo's and Chung Ah-ch'eng's *Ch'i wang*". *Asian Culture Quarterly* 15.4 (Winter 1987): 41–62.

———. "Reinventing China: Cultural Exploration in Contemporary Chinese Fiction". *Issues and Studies* 25.8 (August 1989): 29–53.

Huters, Theodore. "Speaking of Many Things: Food, Kings, and the National Tradition in A Cheng's 'The Chess King'." *Modern China* 14.4 (October 1988): 388–418.

Kinkley, Jeffrey C. "Shen Congwen's Legacy in Chinese Literature of the 1980s". In *From May Fourth to June Fourth: Fiction and Film in Twentieth-Century China*, edited by Ellen Widmer and David Der-wei Wang. Cambridge, MA and London: Harvard University Press, 1993. 71–106.

Knapp, Bettina Liebowitz. "Chapter 10: Cheng's 'The King of the Trees': Exile and the Chinese Reeducation Process". *Exile and the Writer: Exoteric and Esoteric Experiences: A Jungian Approach*. University Park, Pennsylvania: The Pennsylvania State University, 1991. 213–231.

Lee, Leo Ou-fan. "The Crisis of Culture". In *China Briefing 1990*, edited by Anthony J. Kane. Boulder: Westview Press, 1990. 83–105.

Li, Qingxi. "Searching for Roots: Anticultural Return in Mainland Chinese Literature of the 1980s". In *Chinese Literature in the Second Half of a Modern Century: A Critical Survey*, edited by Pang-yuan Chi and David Der-wei Wang. Bloomington and Indianapolis: Indiana University Press, 2000. 110–123.

Louie, Kam. "The Short Stories of A Cheng: Daoism, Confucianism and Life". *The Australian Journal of Chinese Affairs* 18 (July 1987): 1–13.

McDougall, Bonnie S. "Introduction". In *Three Kings: Three Stories from Today's China*, written by A Cheng, and translated by Bonnie S. McDougall. London: Collins Harvill, 1990. 7–25.

Rayns, Tony. "The New Chinese Cinema: An Introduction". In *King of the Children*, by Chen Kaige and Wan Zhi. London and Boston: Faber and Faber, 1989.

Sullivan, Michael. *Art and Artists of Twentieth-century China*. Berkeley and Los Angeles: University of California Press, 1996.

Yue, Gang. "Chapter 2: Writing Hunger: From Mao to the Dao". *The Mouth That Begs: Hunger, Cannibalism, and the Politics of Eating in Modern China*. Durham and London: Duke University Press, 1999. 145–221.

Zhang, Xudong. *Chinese Modernism in the Era of Reforms: Cultural Fever, Avant-garde Fiction, and the New Chinese Cinema*. Durham and London: Duke University Press, 1997.

Zhong, Acheng. "The First Half of My Life: A Boy from the City Struggling for Survival in Far-away Yunnan". In *Modern Chinese Writers: Self-Portrayals*, interviewed and edited by Helmut Martin. Armonk and London: M. E. Sharpe, Inc., 1992. 106–117.

Zweig, Stefan. "The Royal Game". In *The Royal Game, Amok, Letter from an Unknown Woman*, translated by B. W. Huebsch. New York: The Viking Press, 1946. 8–71.

建議參考書目

王德威，〈棋王如何測量水溝的寬度〉。《眾聲喧嘩：三零與八零年代的中國小說》。台北：遠流出版事業股份有限公司，1988年。頁257–268。

———，〈序論：世俗的技藝——閒話阿城與小說〉。鍾阿城，《遍地風流》。台北：麥田出版，2001年。頁9–30。

杜邁可，〈「中華之道畢竟不頹」：評阿城的《棋王》〉。《九十年代》總第187期（1985年8月號）：頁82–85。

李陀，〈1985〉。《今天》第3、4期（1991年）：頁59–73。

阿城，〈一些話〉。林建法、王景濤編，《中國當代作家面面觀：撕碎、撕碎，撕碎了是拼接》。長春：時代文藝出版社，1991年。頁89–91。

———，〈文化制約着人類〉。洪子誠主編，《中國當代文學史·史料選：1945–1999》。兩冊。武漢：長江文藝出版社，2002年。下卷：頁787–790。

———，〈孫曉雲對阿城〉。阿城、陳村等，《我們拿愛情沒辦法》。上海：上海收穫時代文化有限公司，2004年。頁333–355。

林惺嶽，《中國油畫百年史》。台北：藝術家出版社，2000年。

施叔青，〈與阿城談禪論藝〉。《文壇反思與前瞻》。香港：明窗出版社，1988年。頁189–207。

茨威格，〈象棋的故事〉。《斯蒂芬‧茨威格小說四篇》。北京：人民文學出版社，1979。頁103–131。

馬漢茂，〈阿城的前半生(上)〉。《百姓》(半月刊)，第163期(1988年3月1日)：頁54–55。

———，〈阿城的前半生(中)〉。《百姓》(半月刊)，第164期(1988年3月16日)：頁41–43。

———，〈阿城的前半生(下)〉。《百姓》(半月刊)，第165期(1988年4月1日)：頁34–36。

張頌仁策劃，《星星十年》。香港：漢雅軒，1999年。

黃繼持，〈中國當代文學的文化「尋根」討論述評〉。《文學的傳統與現代》。香港：華漢文化事業出版公司，1988年。頁173–187。

韓少功，〈文學的根〉。洪子誠主編，《中國當代文學史‧史料選：1945–1999》。兩冊。武漢：長江文藝出版社，2002年。下卷：頁779–783。

棋　王

The Chess Master

The station could not have been more chaotic. Thousands of people were all talking at once, and nobody was paying any attention to the temporary slogans mounted on scarlet cloth. They had probably been put up quite a few times already as the paper characters from which they were made were torn from being folded so often. The repeated playing of certain quotations that had been turned into songs over the loudspeakers made everyone feel even more frantic.

I had already seen several of my friends off to settle in the countryside, but now that it was my turn there was nobody to see me off. My parents were both dead and I was alone in the world, so I did not qualify for being allowed to stay in the city as an only son. My parents had collected some black marks while they were alive, and as soon as the movement began they had been overthrown and had died. As all the furniture in the flat carried the aluminium tags of public property it was all taken away, which was only right and proper. I had wandered around, as wild as a wolf, for over a year, but in the end I decided that I had to go. Where I was going the pay would be over twenty *yuan* a month, so I was keen to get there; I made a big effort to get the transfer and in the end it was approved. As the place I was going was very near a foreign country, which meant that the struggles there were supposedly international as well as class ones,

車站是亂得不能再亂，成千上萬的人都在說話。誰也不去注意那條臨時掛起來的大紅布標語。這標語大約掛了不少次，字紙都摺得有些壞。喇叭裏放着一首又一首的語錄歌兒，唱得大家心更慌。

　　我的幾個朋友，都已被我送走插隊，現在輪到我了，竟沒有人來送。父母生前頗有些污點，運動一開始即被打翻死去。家具上都有機關的鋁牌編號，於是統統收走，倒也名正言順。我雖孤身一人，卻算不得獨子，不在留城政策之內。我野狼似的轉悠一年多，終於還是決定要走。此去的地方按月有二十幾元工資，我便很嚮往，爭了要去，居然就批了。因為所去之地與別國相鄰，鬥爭之中除了階級，尚有國際，出身孬一些，組織上不太放心。我爭得這個

my dicey family background caused some worries to the organisation people. Needless to say, I was delighted at having won enough of their confidence to be given this privilege. What was even more important was over twenty *yuan* a month, more than I could possibly get through by myself. The only fly in the ointment was having nobody to see me off, so I pushed my way into the carriage to find somewhere to sit down and let the thousands of people on the platform take their leave of each other.

The windows on the side of the carriage next to the platform were already crammed with young leavers from many different schools leaning outside, joking or crying. The windows on the other side faced south, so that the winter sunlight slanting in through them was shining coolly on the many bottoms on the northern side of the carriage. The luggage racks on both sides were alarmingly full. As I walked along, looking for my numbered seat, I noticed a thin and wiry student sitting by himself with his arms in his sleeves. He was gazing out of the window at an empty carriage on the southern side of the station.

As it happened, my place was in the same group of seats as him, facing but not directly opposite. I sat down and put my hands in my sleeves too. The student took a glance at me then his eyes suddenly lit up. "Would you like a game of chess?" he asked, giving me a start.

"I can't play," I replied with a quick gesture.

He looked at me with disbelief. "With long thin fingers like that you must be a chess player. I'm sure you can play. Come on, let's have a game. I've got a set with me." As he spoke he sat up to take his satchel down from the hook by the window and started rummaging about in it.

"I only know the most basic moves," I replied. "Isn't there anyone here to see you off ?"

信任和權利，歡喜是不用説的，更重要的是，每月二十幾元，一個人如何用得完？只是沒人來送，就有些不耐煩，於是先鑽進車廂，想找個地方坐下，任憑站台上千萬人話別。

車廂裏靠站台一面的窗子已經擠滿各校的知青，都探出身去説笑哭泣。另一面的窗子朝南，冬日的陽光斜射進來，冷清清地照在北邊兒眾多的屁股上。兩邊兒行李架上塞滿了東西。我走動着找我的座位號，卻發現還有一個精瘦的學生孤坐着，手攏在袖管兒裏，隔窗望着車站南邊兒的空車皮。

我的座位恰與他在一個格兒裏，是斜對面兒，於是就坐下了，也把手攏在袖裏。那個學生瞄了我一下，眼裏突然放出光來，問：「下棋嗎？」倒嚇了我一跳，急忙擺手説：

「不會！」

他不相信地看着我説：「這麼細長的手指頭，就是個捏棋子兒的，你肯定會。來一盤吧，我帶着家伙呢。」説着就抬身從窗枱上取下書包，往裏掏着。

我説：「我只會馬走日，象走田。你沒人送嗎？」

By now he had his chess set out and had put it on the little table, which was too small for the plastic board. After a moment's thought he rearranged the board sideways on. "Doesn't matter. Play all the same. Come on, you go first. Would you like me to allow you a handicap?"

I burst out laughing. "Is there nobody seeing you off ? How can we play chess in this chaos?"

"Why the hell should I need anyone to see me off ?" he replied as he set the last piece in place. "I'm going where there's food to eat, so why all this crying and snivelling? Come on, you go first."

It all seemed very odd to me, but I still picked up one of my cannons and moved it to the centre line. Before I had the time to put it down he moved his knight, rapping the piece down on the board even faster than I could put mine down, so I deliberately moved my cannon past the centre line.

"And you tell me you don't know how to play!" he said, glaring at my chin. "That opening of taking your cannon one past the centre line I've only ever come across from a player in Zhengzhou, and he damn near beat me. Taking the cannon to the centre line is an old opening; it looks impressive and very safe too. Your move."

I didn't know what move to make, so my hand hovered over the board. He surveyed the whole game without saying or showing anything then put his hands back in his sleeves.

At that very moment the carriage was thrown into chaos as a whole crowd of people pushed inside and waved through the windows to people outside. I stood up and looked out at the platform, where there was a seething, shouting mass of people. The train suddenly jolted, whereupon a groan went up from the crowd and there were sobs everywhere. I felt a shove in my back and looked round to see him

他已把棋盒拿出來，放在茶几上。塑料棋盤卻攔不下，他想了想，就橫擺了，説：「不礙事，一樣下。來來來，你先走。」

我笑起來，説：「你沒人嗎？這麼亂，下什麼棋？」

他一邊碼好最後一個棋子，一邊説：「我他媽要誰送？去的是有飯吃的地方，鬧得這麼哭哭啼啼的。來，你先走。」

我奇怪了，可還是拈起炮，往當頭上一移。我的棋還沒移到，他的馬卻「啪」的一聲跳好，比我還快。我就故意將炮移過當頭的地方停下。

他很快地看了一眼我的下巴，説：「你還説不會？這炮二平六的開局，我在鄭州遇見一個名手，就是這麼走，險些輸給他。炮二平五當頭炮，是老開局，可有氣勢，而且是最穩的。嗯？你走。」

我倒不知怎麼走了，手在棋盤上游移着。他不動聲色地看着整個棋盤，又把手袖起來。

就在這時，車廂亂了起來。好多人擁進來，隔着玻璃往外招手。我就站起身，也隔着玻璃往北看月台上。站上的人都擁到車廂前，都在叫，亂成一片。車身忽地一動，人群「嗡」地一下，哭聲四起。我的背被誰捅了一下，回頭一看，他一手護着棋盤，説：「沒你

shielding the paper board with his arm as he said, "That's no way to play. Get a move on." I hadn't any interest in playing chess, and was besides feeling rather miserable, so I took a tough line with him: "I'm stopping. This is no time for chess." He gave me a look of horror before he suddenly understood. His body relaxed again and he said no more.

The carriage calmed down again after the train had been going for a while, and when hot water was brought along everyone got out their mugs and asked for some. When my neighbour had filled his mug, he asked, "Whose chess set is that? Get it out of the way so we can put our mugs down." "Would you like a game?" the other asked pathetically. "I'm so bored I might just as well," the fellow who wanted to put his mug down replied. The chess player perked up and quickly set the pieces out. "What do you mean, setting the board sideways on like that? You can't see what's happening." "Make do," he replied. "When you watch a game you watch it sideways on. You can have first move." His opponent picked up a piece with an experienced hand and said, "I'll move my cannon into the centre." The chess player sent his knight into action, whereupon his opponent took one of his pawns. At once the chess player took his opponent's cannon with his knight. I didn't find this very conventional opening at all interesting. Besides, chess did not mean very much to me anyhow. I turned away.

A schoolmate of mine came by, apparently looking for someone. As soon as he saw me he said, "Come on. There are three of us and we need a fourth. You!" I shook my head, knowing that they wanted to play cards. My fellow student came into our section and was just going to hand me off when he shouted, "What are you doing here, Chess Maniac? Your sister's been searching for you high and low. I told her I hadn't seen you—it never occurred to me that you'd be hiding here in our school's carriage as quiet as a mouse. Look at you, playing again."

這麼下棋的，走哇！」我實在沒心思下棋，而且心裏有些酸，就硬硬地説：「我不下了。這是什麼時候！」他很驚愕地看着我，忽然像明白了，身子軟下去，不再説話。

車開了一會兒，車廂開始平靜下來。有水送過來，大家就掏出缸子要水。我旁邊的人打了水，説：「誰的棋？收了放缸子。」他很可憐的樣子，問：「下棋嗎？」要放缸子的人説：「反正沒意思，來一盤吧。」他就很高興，連忙碼好棋子。對手説：「這橫着算怎麼回事兒？沒法兒看。」他搓着手説：「湊合了，平常看棋的時候，棋盤不等於是橫着的？你先走。」對手很老練地拿起棋子兒，嘴裏叫着：「當頭炮。」他跟着跳上馬。對手馬上把他的卒吃了，他也立刻用馬吃了對方的炮。我看這種簡單的開局沒有大意思，又實在對象棋不感興趣，就轉了頭。

這時一個同學走過來，像在找什麼人，一眼望到我，就説：「來來來，四缺一，就差你了。」我知道他們是在打牌，就搖搖頭。同學走到我們這一格，正待伸手拉我，忽然大叫：「棋呆子，你怎麼在這兒？你妹妹剛才把你找苦了，我説沒見啊。沒想到你在我們學校這節車廂裏，氣兒都不吭一聲兒。你瞧你瞧，又下上了。」

The Chess Maniac blushed as he replied with evident bad temper, "Do you have to interfere with everything, even my chess? Get lost!" He started urging the man next to me to play again. Only now did I realise that there was something familiar about the voice. "Is that Wang Yisheng?" I asked my fellow student. "Don't you know him?" my fellow student said, staring at me with amazement. "Where've you been all your life? Don't you know about the Chess Maniac?" "I know that the Chess Maniac is called Wang Yisheng, but I didn't realise that he's Wang Yisheng." I took a closer look at the lean and wiry student. Wang Yisheng forced himself to smile, but did not take his eyes off the game.

Wang Yisheng was a name to be reckoned with. My school had often held chess tournaments with other local middle schools, and from these a number of top players had emerged. They used to have challenge matches that Wang Yisheng won almost every time. As I don't like chess I never paid any attention to chess champions and all that, but as the chess fans in my class were always talking about Wang Yisheng even I knew something about him. I knew that his nickname was the Chess Maniac. He was, of course, a brilliant chess player, and on top of that he was one of the best students in his year. It seemed reasonable enough that a good chess player would have a head for maths, but I simply could not believe some of the stupid things Wang Yisheng was supposed to have done. I thought those were just sensational things made up for the sake of a good story. Later on, after the "cultural revolution" had started, the news had gone round one day that he had got into serious trouble while away from home "exchanging revolutionary experience" and been sent back under escort to his school. I expressed my doubts about whether the Chess Maniac could possibly have gone off on an exchange of revolutionary experience. Everything I had heard about him before made it obvious

棋呆子紅了臉，沒好氣兒地說：「你管天管地，還管我下棋？走，該你走了。」就催促我身邊的對手。我這時聽出點音兒來，就問同學：「他就是王一生？」同學睜了眼，說：「你不認識他？唉呀，你白活了。你不知道棋呆子？」我說：「我知道棋呆子就是王一生，可不知道王一生就是他。」說着，就仔細看着這個精瘦的學生。王一生勉強笑一笑，只看着棋盤。

王一生簡直大名鼎鼎。我們學校與旁邊幾個中學常常有學生之間的象棋廝殺，後來拚出幾個高手。幾個高手之間常擺擂台，漸漸地，幾乎每次冠軍就都是王一生了。我因為不喜歡象棋，也就不去關心什麼象棋冠軍，但王一生的大名，卻常被班上幾個棋篓子供在嘴上，我也就對其事迹略聞一二，知道王一生外號棋呆子，棋下得很神不用說，而且在他們學校那一年級裏數理成績總是前數名。我想棋下得好而有個數學腦子，這很合情理，可我又不信人們說的那些王一生的呆事，覺得不過是大家尋逸聞鄙事以快言論罷了。後來運動起來，忽然有一天大家傳說棋呆子在串連時犯了事兒，被人押回學校了。我對棋呆子能出去串連表示懷疑，因為以前大家對他的描述說明他不可能解決串連時的吃喝問題。可大

that he could not possibly have coped with feeding himself when away. But they all insisted that he really had gone. As he played chess all the time he had been spotted by someone who travelled around with him and kept giving him small sums of money that he pocketed without asking any questions. Only later did it emerge that wherever he went the Maniac would squeeze into the place to watch the chess. After watching a game he always pushed the loser aside and played with the winner. At first nobody would play against him as he looked very nondescript, but he kept on insisting until in the end they agreed. After the first few moves his opponent would start sweating slightly but still be talking tough. The Maniac would say nothing, but move so fast that he seemed to be leaving himself no time to think. Once his rival had shut up and the circle of spectators had become so absorbed in thinking about the game that they stopped kibitzing, the Maniac's travelling companion started picking pockets. By then everyone was too absorbed in the game to notice that their wallets had changed hands. In the third game they would all be scratching their heads. The Maniac would now be the chess champion, calling out over and over again for more challenges. Anyone who was not willing to call him best would sit down and have it out with him, but they lost every time. Later on a whole crowd would play against him together, all talking at once. The Maniac would not be flustered by this, but would urge them all to go away as when there were too many players on the other side they tended to quarrel over what moves to make. This was how the Maniac sometimes played nonstop all day. A row would break out when the spectators noticed that their wallets had gone. As time went on a few sensible people started keeping a discreet eye on things. When they noticed a man lifting wallets they said nothing at the time, only raising a hue and cry when the man came back to fetch the Maniac that evening. The pickpocket and the Maniac were both tied up and interrogated by the Rebels. [1] The Maniac was

---

[1] A faction in the culture revolution.

家說呆子確實去串連了，因為老下棋，被人瞄中，就同他各處走，常常送他一點兒錢，他也不問，只是收下。後來才知道，每到一處，呆子必然擠地頭看下棋。看上一盤，必然把輸家擠開，與贏家殺一盤。初時大家看他其貌不揚，不與他下。他執意要殺，於是就殺。幾步下來，對方出了小汗，嘴卻不軟。呆子也不說話，只是出手極快，像是連想都不想。待到對方對於閉了嘴，連一圈兒觀棋的人也要慢慢思索棋路而不再支招兒的時候，與呆子同行的人就開始摸包兒。大家正看得緊張，哪裏想到錢包已經易主？待三盤下來，眾人都摸頭。這時呆子倒成了棋主，連問可有誰還要殺？有那不服的，就坐下來殺，最後仍是無一盤得利。後來常常是眾人齊做一方，七嘴八舌與呆子對手。呆子也不忙，反倒促眾人快走，因為師傅多了，常為一步棋如何走自家爭吵起來。就這樣，在一處呆子可以連殺上一天，後來有那觀棋的人發覺錢包丟了，鬧嚷起來。慢慢有幾個有心計的人暗中觀察，看見有人掏包，也不響，之後見那人晚上來邀呆子走，就發一聲喊，將扒手與呆子一齊綁了，由造反隊審。呆子糊糊塗

very vague: all he could say was that someone kept giving him money. He supposed it was because he was sorry for him, and said he didn't know where the money came from. All he cared about was playing chess. Seeing how stupid he looked, the chief interrogator ordered him sent back under escort. The story spread at once through all the schools.

Later I heard that in the Maniac's view there were not enough good players to be found on the streets in other provinces, which meant that he could not improve his skills. He therefore asked people to get the city's most famous players to give him a game locally. One of his fellow students took the Maniac to meet his father who was supposed to be one of the best players in the country. When the master met the Maniac he said very little, but set out a game in its closing stages that had been handed down from the Song Dynasty and asked the Maniac to move. The Maniac studied the game for a long time, then explained move by move how he would have won the game for the ancient master. This so astonished the modern master that he wanted to take the Maniac as his pupil. The Maniac's question "Could you have got out of that?" had taken him by surprise and left him with no response except to admit, "I haven't worked it out yet." "Then why should I be your pupil?" the Maniac had asked. The master had been forced to ask the Maniac to clear off, and afterwards he had said to his son, "That schoolmate of yours is arrogant and conceited. Chess-playing ability's connected with character, and if he carries on like that his talent is bound to go to the bad too." He had then recited some of the latest Supreme Directives and gone on about how strong his talent for chess would be if only he would study properly.

塗，只說別人常給他錢，大約是可憐他，也不知錢如何來，自己只是喜歡下棋。審主看他呆相，就命人押了回來，一時各校傳為逸事。

後來聽說呆子認為外省馬路棋手高手不多，不能長進，就託人找城裏名手近戰。有個同學就帶他去見自己的父親，據說是國內名手。名手見了呆子，也不多說，只擺一副據傳是宋時留下的殘局，要呆子走。呆子看了半晌，一五一十道來，替古人贏了。名手很驚奇，要收呆子為徒。不料呆子卻問：「這殘局你可走通了？」名手沒反應過來，就說：「還未通。」呆子說：「那我為什麼要做你的徒弟？」名手只好請呆子開路，事後對自己的兒子說：「你這個同學桀驁不遜，棋品連着人品，照這樣下去，棋品必劣。」又舉了一些最新指示，說若能好好學習，棋鋒必健。

Later on the Maniac had got to know an old man who collected waste paper. He only beat the old man in one game during three days of solid chess. The Maniac had insisted on saving the old man from working by tearing down handwritten wallposters for him to sell. One day he had unfortunately torn down a call to arms that had just been posted by one of the Rebel groups and been arrested. The Rebels had falsely accused him of belonging to their opponents' faction, accused them of plotting and conspiracy, and said that they would have to be punished for their intolerable crime. Their opponents had then arranged his rescue and counter-attacked the previous Rebels in the Maniac's name. When the Maniac's name, Wang Yisheng, was plastered all over the streets many revolutionary warriors who had come from other provinces to fetch the scriptures then found out that Wang Yisheng was a chess freak. He was invited to visit their provinces to meet some of the great players who roamed around the country. And although he lost as many games as he won his play became better and better. It was a pity that the whole of China was absorbed in revolution at the time: goodness only knows what the Maniac might have achieved in other circumstances.

As the man sitting next to me now realised that his opponent was Wang Yisheng he did not say another word to him. Wang Yisheng was cast into very low spirits. "Your own sister came to see you off, but instead of having the decency to say a few words to your family you had to grab hold of me to play chess," I said. "How was I to know what my people would be doing?" Wang Yisheng replied, looking at me. "People like you are used to the easy life. There are a lot of things in the world you wouldn't understand. I dare say your parents can't bear to see you go." This shook me, and I looked at my hands as I replied, "What parents? They've both kicked the buchet." My fellow student then told him a well-spiced version of my story, which irritated me. "I lose my parents," I said, "and for you it's just a good story."

　　後來呆子認識了一個撿爛紙的老頭兒，被老頭兒連殺三天而僅贏一盤。呆子就執意要替老頭兒去撕大字報紙，不要老頭兒勞動。不料有一天撕了某造反團剛貼的「檄文」，被人拿獲，又被這造反團栽誣於對立派，說對方「施陰謀，弄詭計」，必討之，而且是可忍，孰不可忍！對立派又陰使人偷出呆子，用了呆子的名義，對先前的造反團反戈一擊。一時呆子的大名「王一生」貼得滿街都是，許多外省來取經的革命戰士許久才明白王一生原來是個棋呆子，就有人請了去外省會一些江湖名手。交手之後，各有勝負，不過呆子的棋據說是越下越精了。只可惜全國忙於革命，否則呆子不知會有什麼造就。

　　這時，我旁邊的人也明白對手是王一生，連說不下了。王一生便很沮喪。我說：「你妹妹來送你，你也不知道和家裏人說說話兒，倒拉着我下棋！」王一生看着我說：「你哪兒知道我們這些人是怎麼回事兒？你們這些人好日子過慣了，世上不明白的事兒多着呢！你家父母大約是捨不得你走了？」我怔了怔，看着手說：「哪兒來父母，都死毬了。」我的同學就添油加醋地敘了我一番，我有些不耐煩，說：「我家死人，你倒有了故事了。」

Wang Yisheng thought for a moment before asking me what I had been living on for the last two years. "I've got by from one day to the next," I replied. "How?" Wang Yisheng asked, fixing his gaze on me. I did not answer. After a silence Wang Yisheng sighed again and said, "Getting by isn't easy. If you've had nothing to eat for a day your chess goes to pieces. Say what you like, I bet your family lived well when your parents were alive." I wasn't going to give in. "You're only making those sarcastic remarks because yours are still alive."

Seeing that the situation was turning ugly my fellow student tried to change the subject. "There's nobody here who's a match for you, Maniac," he said. "Come and play cards with us." "Cards are nothing, " replied the Maniac with a smile. "I could beat the lot of you in my sleep. " "I' ve heard that you can go without food when you're playing chess," my neighbour said. "Food doesn't matter very much to you when you're caught up in something," I replied. "Probably everyone who achieves something does stupid things like that." Wang Yisheng thought about it, then shook his head. "Not me." With that he started looking out of the window.

As the journey continued I gradually became aware that between Wang Yisheng and me there were the beginnings of mutual trust and of fellow feeling based on similar experience. At the same time we both had our suspicions of each other. He was always asking me about what I'd lived on before we met, and in particular about how I'd got by in the two years since the death of my parents. I told him briefly, but he kept pressing for more detail, especially about food. When, for example, the conversation got round to a day during which I'd eaten nothing he asked, "Did you have nothing at all to eat?" "Nothing at all" was my reply. "So when was the next time you ate?" "Later on I met a fellow student. He was going to need his satchel to carry a lot of stuff, so he turned it upside down to empty it. There was a stale steamed bread roll in it so hard that it shattered when it hit the table. I ate the bits while we talked. But, to be frank with you, I find stale sesame seed more filling than stale steamed bread. They keep you going for longer too."

王一生想了想,對我説:「那你這兩年靠什麼活着?」我説:「混一天算一天。」王一生就看定了我問:「怎麼混?」我不答。呆了一會兒,王一生歎一聲,説:「混可不易。一天不吃飯,棋路都亂。不管怎麼説,你父母在時,你家日子還好過。」我不服氣,説:「你父母在,當然要説風涼話。」

我的同學見話不投機,就岔開説:「呆子,這裏沒有你的對手,走,和我們打牌去吧。」呆子笑一笑,説:「牌算什麼,瞌睡着也能贏你們。」我旁邊兒的人説:「據説你下棋可以不吃飯?」我説:「人一迷上什麼,吃飯倒是不重要的事。大約能幹出什麼事兒的人,總免不了有這種傻事。」王一生想一想,又搖搖頭,説:「我可不是這樣。」説完就去看窗外。

一路下去,慢慢我發覺我和王一生之間,既開始有互相的信任和基於經驗的同情,又有各自的疑問。他總是問我與他認識之前是怎麼生活的,尤其是父母死後的兩年是怎麼混的。我大略地告訴了他,可他又特別在一些細節上詳細地打聽,主要是關於吃。例如講到有一次我一天沒有吃到東西,他就問:「一點兒也沒吃到嗎?」我説:「一點兒也沒有。」他又問:「那你後來吃到東西是在什麼時候?」我説:「後來碰到一個同學,他要用書包裝很多東西,就把書包翻倒過來騰乾淨,裏面有一個乾饅頭,掉在桌上就碎了。我一邊兒和他説話,一邊兒就把這些碎饅頭吃下去。不過,説老實話,乾燒餅比乾饅頭解飽得多,而且頂時候兒。」

He agreed with me about stale sesame seed buns, but immediately put another question to me. "I mean, what time was it when you had the stale steamed bread? After midnight?" "Mm ... no," I said. "It was ten at night." "What did you have to eat the next day?" he asked, which got on my nerves rather. To be frank, I did not want to go over all that again, particularly the details. I felt that the experience had corrupted me. It had been it too sharp a contrast with what I had known before, and always seemed to mock my ideals. "I spent that night at my school friend's house," I explained. "The next morning he bought a couple of fried dough strips and I had one of them. That morning I rushed around helping him with some things and he bought me a meal in the street at noon. I felt awkward about eating at his place again that evening, but then another fellow student came along who insisted on dragging me off to his home when he found out that I had nowhere to stay. Of course, I ate all right that day. Well then? Is there anything else you still want cleared up?"

He smiled. "So you didn't go without food for a whole day as you said just now. You had some steamed bread before midnight: you didn't go without for more than twenty-four hours. Besides, you ate well the next day. Averaged out, your calorie intake for the two days was all right."

"You still sound like a bit of an idiot to me," I replied. "You ought to realise that food isn't just something you need for your stomach. It's a spiritual necessity too. If you don't know where you're going to get your next meal it makes you all the keener to eat, and you get hungry quicker too."

"Did you ever know that kind of pressure on your spirit when your family was still well off?" he asked. "I suppose you didn't have any spiritual needs. Or if you did it was that you wanted things to be better. That's greed. Greed is the mark of people like you."

他同意我關於乾燒餅的見解，可馬上又問：「我是說，你吃到這個乾饅頭的時候是幾點？過了當天夜裏十二點嗎？」我說：「噢，不。是晚上十點吧。」他又問：「那第二天你吃了什麼？」講老實話，我不太願意複述這些事情，尤其是細節。我說：「當天晚上我睡在那個同學家。第二天早上，同學買了兩個油餅，我吃了一個。上午我隨他去跑一些事，中午他請我在街上吃。晚上嘛，我不好意思再在他那兒吃，可另一個同學來了，知道我沒什麼着落，硬拉了我去他家，當然吃得還可以。怎麼樣？還有什麼不清楚？」

他笑了，說：「你才不是你剛才說的什麼『一天沒吃東西』，你十二點以前吃了一個饅頭，沒有超過二十四小時。更何況第二天你的伙食水平不低，平均下來，你兩天的熱量還是可以的。」

我說：「你恐怕還是有些呆！要知道，人吃飯，不但是肚子的需要，而且是一種精神需要。不知道下一頓在什麼地方，人就特別想到吃，而且，餓得快。」

他說：「你家道尚好的時候，有這種精力壓力嗎？有，也只不過是想好上再好，那是饞。饞是你們這些人的特點。」

I accepted that there was something to what he was saying, but couldn't help retorting, "You keep saying 'you', 'you', 'you'. But what sort of person are you yourself?" He immediately started looking everywhere but at me as he replied, "Of course I'm different. The main thing is that when it comes to food my demands are fairly basic. Hey, let's change the subject. Do you really not like playing chess? 'How may melancholy be dispelled, save through chess!'"

"What are you so melancholy about?" I asked, looking at him. He still would not look at me. "I'm not melancholy, not at all. Melancholy's a delicacy for bloody gentlemen of letters. People like us aren't melancholy. At most we get a bit fed up. How may being fed up be dispelled save through chess."

Seeing how interested he was in food I watched him as he ate. When the train crew delivered food to the carriages in which we educated youngsters were travelling, his mind no longer seemed to be on chess and he became slightly uneasy. On hearing the clatter of aluminium food boxes as the people in front of us collected their meals, he would usually close his eyes and shut his mouth tight as if he were feeling nauseous. He would start eating fast the moment he got his meal, his Adam's apple regularly contracting and his facial muscles, tensed. He would often pause so that he could use his forefinger to push all the grains of rice and the soup grease round his mouth and on his chin into his mouth. Any grain of rice that fell on his clothes he would lift into his mouth with his fingers and if he did not get a firm hold on a grain and let in fall from his clothes to the floor, his feet stopped moving at once as he leaned over to find it. If he caught my eyes when doing this he would slow down. After he had finished eating he sucked his chopsticks clean then filled his bowl with warm water, after which he would first drink all the oil floating on the top then sip the rest, a little at a time, with the air of someone who has safely reached his haven.

我承認他說得有些道理，禁不住問他：「你總在說你們、你們，可你算什麼人？」他迅速看着其他地方，只是不看我，說：「我當然不同了。我主要是對吃要求得比較實在。唉，不說這些了，你真的不喜歡下棋？何以解憂？唯有象棋。」

我瞧着他說：「你有什麼憂？」他仍然不看我，「沒有什麼憂，沒有。『憂』這玩意兒，是他媽文人的佐料兒。我們這種人，沒有什麼憂，頂多有些不痛快。何以解不痛快？唯有象棋。」

我看他對吃很感興趣，就注意他吃的時候。列車上給我們這幾詳知青車廂送飯時，他若心思不在下棋上，就稍稍有些不安。聽見前面大家拿吃時鋁盒的碰撞聲，他常常閉上眼，嘴巴緊緊收着，倒好像有些噁心。拿到飯後，馬上就開始吃，吃得很快，喉節一縮一縮的，臉上繃滿了筋。常常突然停下來，很小心地將嘴邊或下巴上的飯粒兒和湯水油花兒用整個兒食指抹進嘴裏。若飯粒兒落在衣服上，就馬上一按，拈進嘴裏。若一個沒按住，飯粒兒由衣服上掉下地，他也立刻雙腳不再移動，轉了上身找。這時候他若碰上我的目光，就放慢速度。吃完以後，他把兩隻筷子舔了，拿水把飯盒沖滿，先將上面一層油花吸淨，然後就帶着安全抵岸的神色小口小口地呷。

Once, when he was lightly drumming on the table with his left hand while playing chess, a dried-up grain of rice started dancing quietly on it. He spotted it at once, quickly popping it into his mouth. At once his jaw muscles began to bulge. I knew how easily such dried-up grains of rice can get stuck between you molars so fast that your tongue cannot dislodge them, and indeed it was not long before he was digging around inside his mouth with his fingers. When he had finally chewed the grain up he gulped it down with a big drink of water. His Adam's apple only moved very slowly and there were tears in his eyes. When it came to food he was reverent and very painstaking. At times you even felt a little sorry for the rice that he ate up so completely that not the slightest scrap was left over. There was something rather merciless about it.

Throughout the train journey I watched him playing chess and noticed that while he was just as painstaking about it he was also a lot more generous. He would often start setting the pieces out again and say "Let's have another game" before we had even realised that the situation in the original one was hopeless. Some people would not accept that they were beaten and would insist on playing the game out, as if with a little bit of luck they could get off the death sentence he hinted at. He was glad to accommodate them and destroy them in four or five moves, saying with a touch of mockery, "I was trying to give you a bit of face, but you would have to hear me say 'Checkmate'. Are you hooked on it?"

Whenever I saw him eating I was reminded of Jack London's story *Love of Life*, and in the end I told him the plot when he was sipping his hot water at the end of a meal. As I had known hunger I was particularly affected by the feeling of hunger in the story. He stopped drinking the water, holding the food box to his lips and not moving a muscle as he listened. He was silent for a long time after I had finished,

有一次，他在下棋，左手輕輕地叩茶几。一粒乾縮了的飯粒兒也輕輕跳着。他一下注意到了，就迅速將那個乾飯粒兒放進嘴裏，腮上立刻顯出筋絡。我知道這種乾飯粒兒很容易嵌到槽牙裏，巴在那兒，舌頭是趕它不出的。果然，呆了一會兒，他就伸手到嘴裏去摳。終於嚼完和着一大股口水，「咕」地一聲兒咽下去，喉節慢慢移下來，眼睛裏有了淚花。他對吃是虔誠的，而且很精細。有時你會可憐那些飯被他吃得一個渣兒都不剩，真有點兒慘無人道。

我在火車上一直看他下棋，發現他同樣是精細的，但就有氣度得多。他常常在我們還根本看不出已是敗局時就開始重碼棋子，說：「再來一盤吧。」有的人不服輸，非要下完，總覺得被他那樣暗示死刑存些僥幸，他也奉陪，用四五步棋逼死對方，說：「非要聽『將』，有癮？」

我每看到他吃飯，就回想起傑克‧倫敦的《熱愛生命》，終於在一次飯後他小口呷湯時講了這個故事，我因為有過飢餓的經驗，所以特別渲染了故事中的飢餓感覺。他不再喝湯，只是把飯盒端在嘴邊兒，一動不動地聽我講。我講完了，他呆了許久，凝視着飯盒裏的水，

gazing at the water in his box and quietly sipping a mouthful of it before looking at me very solemnly and saying, "He was right. Of course he had to keep the biscuit under his mattress. From the way you tell it his fear after losing his food was mental illness. No, he was right. You can't take the man in the book that way. Jack ... Jack what? Oh yes, Jack London, the swine. A man with a full belly who didn't know what the hungry suffer."

I told him at once what sort of person Jack London had been. "Yes," he replied, "there's no getting out of it. From what you say Jack London got famous after that. He can't possibly have had to worry about where his next meal was coming from. He'd have sat there smoking a cigarette as he wrote his stories mocking hunger." "Jack London never, ever mocked hunger," I protested. "He was ..." "What do you mean, never mocked?" he interrupted impatiently. "Turning someone who had a very clear idea of hunger into a mental case: I don't like that."

All I could do was to give a wry smile and say no more. But whenever there was nobody to play chess with him he'd say, "Hey, will you tell me another story about food. That Jack London one was terrific." "It's not a story about food at all," I replied with irritation. "It's a story about life. You really deserve to be known as the Chess Maniac." He did not know what to do, probably because of the expression on my face. Something welled up inside me at this. I did, after all, like him. "Okay. Have you heard Balzac's *Le cousin Pons*?" He shook his head, so I told him about greedy old Pons. When he had heard it through he surprised me by saying, "That story's no good. It's a story about greed, not about food. If Pons had only eaten and not been greedy he wouldn't have died. I don't like that story." Then he realised what he had just said and quickly added, "No, I don't dislike it. But foreigners are never the same as us. There's something that comes between us. Let me tell you a story."

輕輕吸了一口，才很嚴肅地看着我説：「這個人是對的。他當然要把餅乾藏在褥子底下。照你講，他是對失去食物發生精神上的恐懼，是精神病？不，他有道理，太有道理了。寫書的人怎麼可以這麼理解這個人呢？傑……傑什麼？嗯，傑克‧倫敦，這個小子他媽真是飽漢子不知餓漢子飢。」

我馬上指出傑克‧倫敦是一個如何如何的人。他説：「是呀，不管怎麼樣，像你説的，傑克‧倫敦後來出了名，肯定不愁吃的，他當然會叼着根煙，寫些嘲笑飢餓的故事。」我説：「傑克‧倫敦絲毫也沒有嘲笑飢餓，他是……」他不耐煩地打斷我説：「怎麼不是嘲笑？把一個特別清楚飢餓是怎麼回事兒的人寫成發了神經，我不喜歡。」

我只好苦笑，不再説什麼。可是一沒人和他下棋了，他就又問我：「嗯？再講個吃的故事？其實傑克‧倫敦那個故事挺好。」我有些不高興地説：「那根本不是個吃的故事，那是一個講生命的故事。你不愧為棋呆子。」大約是我臉上有種表情，他於是不知怎麼辦才好。我心裏有一種東西升上來，我還是喜歡他的，就説：「好吧，巴爾扎克的《邦斯舅舅》聽過嗎？」他搖搖頭。我就又好好兒描述一下邦斯這個老饕。不料他聽完，馬上就説：「這個故事不好，這是一個饞的故事，不是吃的故事。邦斯這個老頭兒若只是吃而不饞，不會死。我不喜歡這個故事。」他馬上意識到這最後一句話，就急忙説：「倒也不是不喜歡。不過洋人總和咱們不一樣，隔着一層。我給你講個故事吧。」

This aroused my interest immediately: even the Chess Maniac knew a story. Leaning back and making himself more comfortable, he said "In the old days," and smiled. "it's always in the bloody old days," he continued, "but anyhow, this story was told by Old Fifth Granny who lived in our courtyard. Well, a long time ago there was this family that never had to worry about where its next meal was coming from. They had grain by the binful and they could eat as much as they wanted to for every meal. They had it cushy. Later on a bride married into the family. She was very capable. She never once burned the rice. It was never too dry or too soft, and it was very satisfying. But every time she cooked a meal she took out a handful of uncooked rice and hid it away...."

At this point I couldn't stop myself interrupting and saying, "That story's so old its teeth have all fallen out. It goes on about how later on, when there was a famine and nobody had anything to eat the young woman brought out the rice she'd been putting away every day, so that her family had enough and she even had some to give to the poor."

He was so surprised he sat bolt upright. "Do you know the story?" he asked, looking at me. "But they never gave the rice to anyone else. Fifth Granny never said anything about that."

"It's only a story to teach little kids frugality," I said with a smile, "and you tell it with such zest. You really are a maniac. It's not a story about eating." He shook his head as he replied, "But it is a story about eating. You have to have food before you can eat. That family had bins and bins of grain. But you mustn't eat everything. You've got to remember that there'll be a time when there'll be nothing to eat. After every meal you ought to be left feeling a bit empty. As the old saying goes, stay half hungry and you'll live to a ripe old age."

我馬上感了興趣：棋呆子居然也有故事！他把身體靠得舒服一些，說：「從前哪。」笑了笑，又說：「老是他媽從前，可這個故事是我們院兒的五奶奶講的。嗯——老輩子的時候，有這麼一家子，吃喝不愁。糧食一囤一囤的，頓頓想吃多少吃多少，嘿，可美氣了。後來呢，娶了個兒媳婦。那真能幹，就沒說把飯做糊過，不乾不稀，特解飽。可這媳婦，每做一頓飯，必抓出一把米藏好……」

聽到這兒，我忍不住插嘴：「老掉牙的故事了，還不是後來遇了荒年，大家沒飯吃，媳婦把每日攢下的米拿出來，不但自家有了，還分給窮人？」

他很驚奇地坐直了，看着我說：「你知道這個故事？可那米沒有分給別人，五奶沒有說分給別人。」

我笑了，說：「這是教育小孩兒要節約的故事，你還拿來有滋有味兒地講，你真是呆子，這不是一個吃的故事。」他搖搖頭，說：「這太是吃的故事了，首先得有飯，才能吃，這家子有一囤一囤的糧食。可光窮吃不行，得記着斷頓兒的時候，每頓都要欠一點兒。老話說『半飢半飽日子長』嘛。」

I wanted to laugh but couldn't: I seemed to have understood something. To get rid of this strange sensation I said, "I'll give you a game, Maniac."

He cheered up at once, pulled himself together, set the pieces out with a noisy clatter, and said, "OK. What's the point in stories about eating? Let's play chess instead." He laughed, "You take first move." Once again I opened by moving my cannon to the centre, he moved his knight out to counter it. I casually made my next move and he quickly moved a pawn forward one space. My mind was not really on the game; I was thinking that he must have read a great deal at middle school. "Have you read Cao Cao's 'Short Song'?" I asked him. "What 'Short Song'?" he said. "Then how did you know the lines, 'How may melancholy be dispelled, save through Du Kang?'" I replied. That shook him. "What's doocan?" he asked. "Du Kang was the man who first made wine," I said, "which is why his name was used to mean wine. You changed 'Du Kang' to 'chess', and that was rather neat." "No," he said, shaking his head, "it was something an old man said. He said it every time I played with him."

I remembered the old man who gathered waste paper in the stories about Wang Yisheng and asked, "Was it the old man who collected waste paper?" "No," he replied, after casting a glance at me. "But the old man who collected waste paper was a good player and I learnt a lot from him." "What sort of man was he, your old wastepaper collector?" I asked with interest. "Why did he collect old paper if he was such a good chess player?" "Playing chess doesn't feed you," he replied with a quiet laugh. "The old man had to gather his paper if he wanted to eat. I don't know what he was originally. Once I lost some sheets of paper I'd copied some games out on. I thought I must have chucked them out as rubbish, so I went to the rubbish dump to search for them. As I was turning the rubbish over this old man pushed his

我想笑但沒笑出來，似乎明白了一些什麼。為了打消這種異樣的感觸，就說：「呆子，我跟你下棋吧。」

他一下高興起來，緊一緊手臉，啪啪啪就把棋碼好，說：「對，說什麼吃的故事，還是下棋。下棋最好，何以解不痛快？唯有下象棋。啊？哈哈哈，你先走。」我又是當頭炮，他隨後把馬跳好。我隨便動了一個子兒子，他很快地把兵移前一格兒。我並不真心下棋，心想他念到中學，大約是讀過不少書的，就問：「你讀過曹操的〈短歌行〉？」他說：「什麼〈短歌行〉？」我說：「那你怎麼知道『何以解憂，唯有杜康』？」他愣了，問：「杜康是什麼？」我說：「杜康是一個造酒的人，後來也就代表酒，你把杜康換成象棋，倒也風趣。」他擺了一下頭，說：「啊，不是。這句話是一個老頭兒說的，我每回和他下棋，他總說這句。」

我想起了傳聞中的撿爛紙的老頭兒，就問：「是撿爛紙的老頭兒嗎？」他看了我一眼，說：「不是。不過，撿爛紙的老頭兒棋下得好，我在他那兒學到不少東西。」我很感興趣地問：「這老頭兒是個什麼人？怎麼下得一手好棋還撿爛紙？」他很輕地笑了一下，說：「下棋不當飯。老頭兒要吃飯，還得撿爛紙。可不知他以前是什麼人。有一回，我抄的幾張棋譜不知怎麼找不到了，以為當垃圾倒出去了，就到垃圾站去翻。正翻着，這個老頭推着筐過來了，指着我說：

basket over towards me. 'You're a big lad,' he said, and he pointed at me, 'so what are you trying to take my living off me for?' I told him I wasn't; I was looking for some things I'd lost. He asked me what. I ignored him, but he kept on asking. 'Money? A bank book? Marriage lines?' I had to tell him it was some transcriptions of chess games, and just as I was explaining I found them. Then he told me to show him them. He read them through in next to no time by the light of the street lamp, then said, 'There's nothing to these games.' I told him they'd been played in some previous city tournaments. 'No tournaments anywhere are any use,' he said. 'Just look. What sort of chess strategies are these? The idiots!' I thought I might be onto some kind of genius, so I asked him what the moves ought to be. He talked through a whole game, and it was obvious straight away that he was something special, so I asked him to give me a game. He made me say my move first. There we were, playing chess in our heads on the rubbish dump. I lost five games in a row. The old man's first few moves didn't sound like anything much, but his games were dead cunning and really vicious. He struck like lightning. He knew how to set a trap and how to spring it fast so you couldn't get out. After that we used to play mental chess by the rubbish dump every day. I used to think his games over every day when I went home. Eventually I managed to draw a game with him, and even win one. Actually, we'd only made a dozen or so moves in the game I won. The old man tapped the ground for quite a long time with his wire scavenging claw, sighed, and said, 'You've won!' I was very excited, and told him straight that I wanted to go and see him at his place. He gave me a dirty look, said, 'You're too full of yourself,' and told me to wait for him at the same place the next day.

"Well, I went there he next day, and I saw him from a long way off. He was pushing his basket along. When he got close to me he brought a small cloth bundle out of the basket and put it in my hand. He said

『你個大小伙子，怎麼搶我的買賣？』我說不是，是找丟了的東西，他問什麼東西，我沒搭理他。可他問個不停：『錢？存摺兒？結婚帖子？』我只好說是棋譜，正說着，就找着了。他說叫他看看。他在路燈底下挺快就看完了，說：『這棋沒根哪』。我說這是以前市裏的象棋比賽。可他說：『哪兒的比賽也沒用，你瞧這，這叫棋路？狗腦子。』我心想怕是遇上異人了，就問他當怎麼走，老頭兒嘩嘩說了一通譜兒，我一聽，真的不凡，就提出要跟他下一盤。老頭讓我先說。我們倆就在垃圾站下盲棋，我是連輸五盤。老頭兒棋路猛聽頭幾步，沒什麼，可着子真陰真狠，打閃一般，網得開，收得又緊又快。後來我們見天兒在垃圾站下盲棋，每天回去我就琢磨他的棋路，以後居然跟他平過一盤，還贏過一盤，其實贏的那盤我們一共才走了十幾步。老頭兒用鉛絲扒子敲了半天地面，歎一聲，『你贏了。』我高興了，直說要到他那兒去看看。老頭兒白了我一眼，說，『撐的？！』告訴我明天晚上再在這兒等他。

　　第二天我去了，見他推着筐遠遠來了。到了跟前，從筐裏取出一個小布包，遞到我手上，說這也是譜兒，讓我拿回去，看瞧得懂

there were transcripts of games in it, and I was to take them back with me and find out whether I understood them or not. He also told me that whenever I got stuck in a game I was to go and tell him about it as perhaps he could get me out of it. I hurried back home, opened the bundle up and looked—and I bloody well couldn't understand it either. It was a weird book. Goodness knows when it went back to. It was handwritten, full of notes in the margins, and all patched up. What was in it didn't seem to be about chess at all—it looked as though it was about something completely different.

"When I went to see him the next day and told him I couldn't understand it, he burst out laughing. He said he'd explain a passage to give me a clue. Once he started explaining I had quite a shock. It started off with an opening statement that it was all about sex. I said that it was one to the 'four olds'. [2] What was old, he asked with a sigh. Wasn't the waster paper I collected every day old? But when I took it home I sorted it out and sold it for the money to buy the food to support myself. Wasn't that new? Then he said that China's Taoists talked a lot about the Yin and the Yang. That opening chapter was using male and female to explain the Yin and the Yang. The Yin and the Yang principles sometimes move apart and sometimes join together. You mustn't be too given to winning. If you win too much you break."

I nodded.

"'Win too much and you will break, be too feeble and you will leak away.' The old man said that what was wrong with me was that I was too keen to win. Then he told me that if my opponent was too eager to win I should use soft methods to transform him. While I was transforming him I should be setting up the situation in which to defeat

---

[2] "Old ideas, old culture, old customs and old habits"—all targets of the "cultural revolution".

不。又説哪天有走不動的棋，讓我到這兒來説給他聽聽，興許他就走動了。我趕緊回到家裏，打開一看，還真他媽不懂。這是本異書，也不知是哪朝哪代的，手抄，邊邊角角兒，補了又補。上面寫的東西，不像是説象棋，好像是説另外的什麼事兒。

我第二天又去找老頭兒，説我看不懂，他哈哈一笑，説他先給我説一段兒，提個醒兒。他一開説，把我嚇了一跳。原來開宗明義，是講男女的事兒，我説這是『四舊』。老頭兒歎了，説什麼是舊？我這每天撿爛紙是不是在撿舊？可我回去把它們分門別類，賣了錢，養活自己，不是新？又説咱們中國道家講陰陽，這開篇是借男女講陰陽之氣。陰陽之氣相游相交，初不可太盛，太盛則折。折就是『折斷』的『折』」。

我點點頭。

「『太盛則折，太弱則瀉。』老頭兒説我的毛病是太盛。又説，若對手盛，則以柔化之。可要在化的同時，造成克勢。柔不是弱，

him. Softness isn't weakness. It's containing, drawing in, holding. By holding and transforming your opponent you draw him into the strategy you're setting up. To create this strategic situation you do everything by forcing nothing. Forcing nothing is the Way. It's also the unchangeable nature of chess. Try to change it and it won't be chess. You won't just lose: you won't even be able to play at all. You can't go against the nature of chess, but you have to create your own strategy in every game you play. Once you've sorted out both the nature of chess itself and your own strategy there's nothing you can't do. It really is mysterious, but if you think it over carefully you'll find it's true.

"I told him that what he'd said had really opened my eyes, but how could you be sure of winning at chess when there are so many possibilities? The old man explained that this was what the art of strategy was all about. The essence of strategy is in turning points. If nobody moved it wouldn't be possible to play. But once your opponent moves he can mount an offensive and you can lead him on. If he's any good you can't attack him, so you have to take losses. So he loses a piece and you lose a piece. First you deflect his attack or else find an opening so that you can pin him down. You block his offensive and set up your own. At this point you mustn't be pigheaded about losing pieces. You've got to be ready to adopt your strategy to changing circumstances. One strategy leads into another. You use your strategy to trap his. You have to open things up with a minor strategy, which is absorbed into and turned into your major strategy. They should be so closely intertwined that the other man is helpless.

"The old man told me that all I knew about were traps. I didn't really understand strategies. I could set a trap a long way ahead, but as I had no strategy, I couldn't create the overall climate of a game. But then he said that I had a good head and could work things out.

是容，是收，是含。含而化之，讓對手入你的勢。這勢要你造，需
無為而無不為。無為即是道，也就是棋運之大不可變，你想變，就
不是象棋，輸不用說了，連棋邊兒都沾不上。棋運不可悖，但每局
的勢要自己造。棋運和勢既有，那可就無所不為了。玄是真玄，可
細琢磨，是那麼個理兒。

　　我說，這麼講是真提氣，可這下棋，千變萬化，怎麼才能準贏
呢？老頭兒說這就是造勢的學問了。造勢妙在契機。誰也不走子兒，
這棋沒法兒下。可只要對方一動，勢就可入，就可導。高手你入他很
難，這就要損。損他一個子兒，損自己一個子兒，先導開，或找眼釘
下，止住他的入勢，鋪排下自己的入勢。這時你萬不可死損，勢式要
相機而變。勢式有相因之氣，勢套勢，小勢導開，大勢含而化之，根
連根，別人就奈何不得。

　　老頭兒說我只有套，勢不太明。套可以算出百步之遠，但無
勢，不成氣候。又說我腦子好，有琢磨勁兒，後來輸我的那一盤，

The game he lost to me had been when his strategy had been ruined: it would just have been messing about to have gone on playing.

"Then he told me that as he wasn't long for this world and had no kids of his own he wanted to pass everything on to me now that we'd met. I asked him why he didn't make a living out of chess as he was so good at it. He sighed and told me that his chess was something handed down by his ancestors, but that they had also taught that you don't play chess to earn your living. Playing chess was to nourish your nature, and your livelihood could damage your nature, which was why you could not be too successful in making a living. Then he said that this teaching had damaged him, because he'd never been taught any skills that could have earned him a living."

"Can there possibly be any difference between the principles of chess and the principles of life?" I asked, astonished. "That's what I said too, and the devil got into me then," said Wang Yisheng. "I started asking him about the world situation. What the old man said was that in chess there were only so many pieces and the board was only so big. It was the same principles, but different situations. You can keep an eye on all the chess pieces, but in the world there are too many things you don't know about. There are brand new handwritten posters every day, and though you can see a bit of what they're up to, you can't fathom it all. The pieces aren't all on the board, so it's a game you can't play."

I went on to ask him about the book of chess games. "I used to carry it about with me all the time and read it over and over again," he said dejectedly. "As you know, I got arrested later on by a Rebel group for tearing down one of their posters. They found the book when they searched me and said it was one of the 'four olds', so they destroyed it, and right in front of my eyes too. Luckily I had the book in my head already, so it didn't matter what they did." Once again I gave a long sigh with him.

就是大勢已破，再下，就是玩了。

老頭兒説他日子不多了，無兒無女，遇見我，就傳給我吧。我説你老人家棋道這麼好，怎麼還幹這種營生呢？老頭兒歎一口氣，説這棋是祖上傳下來，但有訓──『為棋不為生』，為棋是養性，生會壞性，所以生不可太盛。又説他從小沒學過什麼謀生本事，現在想來，倒是訓壞了他。」

我似乎聽明白了一些棋道，可很奇怪，就問：「棋道與生道難道有什麼不同麼？」王一生説：「我也是這麼説，而且魔症起來，問他天下大勢。老頭兒説，棋就是這麼幾個子兒，棋盤就這麼大，無非是道同勢不同，可這子兒你全能看在眼底。天下的事，不知道的太多。這每天的大字報，張張都新鮮，雖看出點道兒，可不能究底。子兒不全擺上，這棋就沒法兒下。」

我就又問那本棋譜。王一生很沮喪地説：「我每天帶在身上，反覆地看。後來你知道，我撕大字報被造反團捉住，書就被他們搜了去，説是『四舊』，給毀了，而且是當着我的面兒毀的。好在書已在我腦子裏，不怕他們。」我就又和王一生感歎了許久。

The train finally arrived, and all us school leavers were taken to the state farm by lorry. People came from all the branch farms to collect us from the farm headquarters. I went to find Wang Yisheng. "We'll have to go our separate ways now, Maniac," I said. "Don't forget our friendship. Whether we've got anything special to do or not, let's keep in contact." He said that of course he would.

　　火車終於到了。所有的知識青年都又被用卡車運到農場。在總場，各分場的人上來領我們。我找到王一生，說：「呆子，要分手了，別忘了交情，有事兒沒事兒，互相走動。」他說當然。

2

The farm was deep in the mountain forests. The work was cutting down trees, burning off the mountainsides, digging holes and replanting. When we weren't planting trees we were growing a little grain. Communications were bad, and transport was inadequate: we often could not even buy paraffin for our lamps. At night with no lights and no fire we'd all get together to shoot our mouths off about anything and everything. Because they were always "cutting off the tails of capitalism" ③ we were living extremely badly. There was only half an ounce of oil for each of us a month, so the moment the food bell rang everyone ran flat out to the kitchen. The people who came in last would only get pumpkins or aubergines boiled in plain water. The vegetables were boiled in big vats and what little oil there was only got added later, so it floated on the surface. There was plenty of rice. The state supplied each of us twenty-one kilos of commercial-grade rice a month. But digging pits in the mountains is heavy work, so without any oil our stomachs swelled up as we ate it. It didn't bother me—it was better than begging. We got over twenty *yuan* a month in pay too, and as I didn't have anyone to worry about at home and hadn't found a girlfriend I bought cigarettes and learned to smoke. The more I did it the worse it got.

---

③ Which meant eliminating all profitable side-line occupations.

這個農場在大山林裏，活計就是砍樹，燒山，挖坑，再栽樹。不栽樹的時候，就種點兒糧食。交通不便，運輸不夠，常常就買不到煤油點燈。晚上黑燈瞎火，大家湊在一起臭聊，天南地北。又因為常割資本主義尾巴，生活就清苦得很，常常一個月每人只有五錢油，吃飯鐘一敲，大家就疾跑如飛。大鍋菜是先煮後攔油，油又少，只在湯上浮幾個大花兒。落在後邊，常常就只能吃清水南瓜或清水茄子。米倒是不缺，國家供應商品糧，每人每月四十二斤。可沒油水，挖山又不是輕活，肚子就越吃越大。我倒是沒什麼，畢竟強似討吃。每月又有二十幾元工薪，家裏沒有人惦記着，又沒有找女朋友，就買了煙學抽，不料越抽越兇。

When the work in the mountains was at its heaviest we were often dropping with exhaustion. I wondered how the Maniac was getting by. He was so skinny. When we all talked in the evening it was usually to eat an imaginary banquet, and it occurred to me that he must be an even more dreadful sight when eating. My father had been a fine cook when he was alive, much better than my mother. He used to invite colleagues round every Sunday just to appreciate his cooking, and I'd become something of a gourmet too, so when it came to this kind of conversation I often took the lead. What I said would get all their cheeks bulging, and they often used to push me to the ground with a great shout. They said that someone like me was a disaster, and the best thing to do would be to slaughter me and fry me up.

In the rainy season we were all busy digging up bamboo shoots on the mountains and catching frogs in the ditches, but because we had no oil it often gave us stomachache. We were always burning off the mountainsides, but when the wild animals ran away in terror it was almost impossible to shoot one. Even if we did get them, they had no fat on them as they spent all their time running: there was no oil to be got out of them. We also caught and ate rats that were about a foot long. As rats eat grain everyone said that rat flesh was the same as human flesh, so that we were as good as eating human flesh. Surely the Maniac must be greedy, I often thought. If the food was really good of course he'd be greedy, and when he was hungry he'd be even greedier. Without greed the eating instinct could never come into play, and it would not be able to find sustenance. Then I went on to wonder whether the idiot was still playing chess. Our branch farm was nearly fifty kilometres from his, making visits difficult, so I did not manage to see him.

In the twinkling of an eye it was summer. I was working in the mountains one day when I saw someone in the distance on the track at the foot of the mountain. Everyone felt that it was a stranger and

山上活兒緊時，常常累翻，就想：呆子不知怎麼幹？那麼精瘦的一個人。晚上大家閑聊，多是精神會餐。我又想，呆子的吃相可能更惡了。我父親在時，炒得一手好菜，母親都比不上他。星期天常邀了同事，專事品嚐，我自然精於此道。因此聊起來，常常是主角，說得大家個個兒腮脹，常常發一聲喊，將我按倒在地上，說像我這樣兒的人實在是禍害，不如宰了炒吃。

下雨時節，大家都慌忙上山去挖筍，又到溝裏捉田雞，無奈沒有油，常常吃得胃酸。山上總要放火，野獸們都驚走了，極難打到。即使打到，野物們走慣了，沒膘，熬不得油。尺把長的老鼠也捉來吃，因鼠是吃糧的，大家說鼠肉就是人肉，也算吃人吧。我又常想，呆子難道不饞？好上加好，固然是饞，其實餓時更饞。不饞，吃的本能不能發揮，也不得寄託。又想，呆子不知還下不下棋。我們分場與他們分場隔着近百里，來去一趟不容易，也就見不着。

轉眼到了夏季。有一天，我正在山上幹活兒，遠遠望見山下小路上有一個人。大家覺得影兒生，就議論是什麼人。有人說是小毛

was arguing about who it was. Someone said it was Little Mao's bloke. Little Mao was an educated girl who had recently got herself a boyfriend in another farm, but nobody had seen him. Little Mao threw down her mattock and rushed over, tripping and stumbling, looking eagerly. Before she could make out who it was I had recognised the stranger as Wang Yisheng, the Chess Maniac. When I shouted to him it gave the rest of them a start. "Has he come to see you?" they all asked. I was very pleased. There were educated youngsters from four cities and provinces in our team, and only a few of them had come with me, so it was natural that none of them knew Wang Yisheng. At the time I was the acting head of a group of three or four of us, so I said, "Let's break up and stop working. But don't go back. Get anything edible you can find on the mountain. Come down when the bell rings and bring it to my place to cook it there. You fetch your rice and bring it over. We'll eat together." They all rushed off into the undergrowth and started searching.

I went jumping and running down the mountain. Wang Yisheng had stopped and looked very happy. "How did you know it was me?" he asked when I was still some distance from him. "I could recognise your crazy look from miles away," I said when I reached him. "Why've you never come to see me?" The clothes on his back were soaked in sweat, his hat was plastered down on his forehead and his face was covered in dust. Only his eyes and teeth shone bright. His lips were engrained with dirt and so dry that they had cracked. "How did you get here?" I asked. "I hitched a lift some of the way and walked for a while. I've been away for a fortnight." This shocked me. "But it's less than fifty kilometres," I said, "how did you take so long?" "I'll tell you all about it when we get back," he replied.

As we talked we reached the brigade headquarters in the valley. Some of the farm's pigs were rushing about, all skinnier than dogs. The place was deserted as it was not yet time to knock off. There was only a muffled clatter from the brigade kitchen.

的男的吧。小毛是隊裏一個女知青，新近在外場找了一個朋友，可誰也沒見過。大家就議論可能是這個人來找小毛，於是滿山喊小毛，說她的漢子來了。小毛丟了鋤，跌跌撞撞跑過來，伸了脖子看。還沒等小毛看好，我卻認出來人是王一生——棋呆子。於是大叫，別人倒嚇了一跳，都問：「找你的？」我很得意。我們這個隊有四個省市的知青，與我同來的不多，自然他們不認識王一生。我這時正代理一個管三四個人的小組長，於是對大家說：「散了，不幹了。大家也別回去，幫我看看山上可有什麼吃的弄點兒，到鐘點兒再下山，拿到我那兒去燒。你們打了飯，都過來一起吃。」大家於是就鑽進亂草裏去尋了。

我跳着跑下山，王一生已經站住，一臉高興的樣子，遠遠地問：「你怎麼知道是我？」我到了他跟前說：「遠遠就看你呆頭呆腦，還真是你。你怎麼老也不來看我？」他跟我並排走着，說：「你也老不來看我呀！」我見他背上的汗浸出衣衫，頭髮已是一綹一綹的，一臉的灰土，只有眼睛和牙齒放光，嘴上也是一層土，幹得起皺，就說：「你怎麼摸來的？」他說：「搭一段兒車，走一段兒路，出來半個月了。」我嚇了一跳，問：「不到百里，怎麼走這麼多天？」他說：「回去細說。」

說話間已經到了溝底隊裏。場上幾隻豬跑來跑去，個個兒瘦得賽狗。還不到下班時間，冷冷清清的，只有隊上伙房隱隱傳來叮叮當當的聲音。

When we reached my dormitory we went straight in. It was not locked as there was nothing surplus to be stolen, and so no need for precautions. I put a basin on the floor and asked him to wait while I fetched a bucket of boiling water for him to wash with. In the kitchen I talked to the cook and found out that as I had already drawn my twenty-five gram of oil for the month I would only be able to have raw vegetables instead of cooked ones from then on. "Got a visitor?" the cook asked. "Sure," I replied. The cook opened a locked cupboard, took out a small spoonful of oil and found a bowl to put it in for me, as well as three long aubergines. "You can come and draw your food tomorrow as usual," he said. "We'll start the day after tomorrow to make it a bit easier for you." I filled my bucket with hot water and took it back to the dormitory.

Wang Yisheng had stripped to his underpants and was washing noisily. When he had finished washing himself he put his dirty clothes into the water to soak, rubbed them one by one, then washed, rinsed, wrung and hung them out to dry on the clothes line by the door. "You're very efficient," I said. "I'm used to it," he said. "I've been looking after myself since I was a kid. A few clothes are no trouble." As he spoke he sat down on the bed and twisted his arm round to scratch his back, moving all his ribs. I got my cigarette out to offer him. He tapped one out with great expertise, lifted it out of the packet with his tongue, and turned it over to put between his lips. I lit his then lit up mine too. He inhaled deeply, raising his shoulders, then slowly blew the smoke out. His whole body swayed. "Not bad at all," he said with a smile. "How's that then?" I said. "Are you a smoker too now? I suppose you're living quite well."

He gazed at the thatched roof then at the pigs milling around by the doorway, after which he looked down and just gently tapped his skinny thighs. It was a long time before be said, "Quite well, really

到了我的宿舍，就直進去。這裏並不鎖門，都沒有多餘的東西可拿，不必防誰。我放了盆，叫他等着，就提桶打熱水來給他洗。到了伙房，與炊事員講，我這個月的五錢油金數領出來，以後就領生菜，不再打熟菜。炊事員問：「來客了？」我說：「可不！」炊事員就打開鎖了的櫃子，舀一小匙油找了個碗盛給我，又拿了三隻長茄子，說：「明天還來打菜吧，從後天算起，方便。」我從鍋裏舀了熱水，提回宿舍。

王一生把衣裳脫了，只剩一條褲衩，呼嚕呼嚕地洗。洗完後，將髒衣服按在水裏泡着，然後一件一件搓，洗好涮好，擰乾晾在門口繩上。我說：「你還挺麻利的。」他說：「從小自己幹，慣了。幾件衣服，也不費事。」說着就在牀上坐下，彎過手臂，去撓後背，肋骨一根根動着。我拿出煙來請他抽。他很老練地敲出一支，舔了一頭兒，倒過來叼着。我先給他點了，自己也點上。他支起肩紳吸進去，慢慢地吐出來，渾身蕩一下，笑了，說：「真不錯。」我說：「怎麼樣？也抽上了？日子過得不錯呀。」

他看看草頂，又看看在門口轉來轉去的豬，低下頭，輕輕拍着淨是綠筋的瘦腿，半晌才說：「不錯，真的不錯。還說什麼呢？糧？錢？

quite well. What should I tell you about? Grain? Money? What else do you want? Quite well, really quite well. How are things with you?" He asked this question through a fog of smoke. "Plenty of money," I replied with a sigh, "plenty of grain. Not bad, but no oil. The mass-produced food gives you stomachache. The main thing is that there's no entertainment. No books, no electricity, no films, It's hard to go anywhere. We're stuck in this valley. It's dead boring."

"You people," he said, looking at me and shaking his head. "You can't say so in as many words, but you all want icing on it. I'm very satisfied. What else do I need? But you, you've been ruined by books. I thought a lot about the two stories you told me on the train and got to like them a lot. You're quite something. You've read a lot. But when it comes down to it, what can reading solve? Yes, you can give everything you've got to keep alive and end up crazy. Later on you get better and you carry on living, but how? Like Pons? He had food and drink and liked having a bit stashed away, but the trouble with him was that he was greedy. If he wasn't being treated to meals he felt miserable. People ought to know when to be satisfied. If you can eat your fill at every meal you're lucky." He fell silent, gazing at his toes as he wiggled them. Then he rubbed the heel of one foot against the back of the other, blew out a mouthful of smoke, and flicked his legs with his fingers.

I wished I had not used oil and things one could do without, such as books and films, to show how fed up I was with the life there. To him these all came above the basic survival line, and he was not bothered about them. I suddenly felt deflated and tending to agree with what he said. Yes, what else did I need? Didn't I think it was fine here? I never had to worry about where my next meal was coming from, and even if my bed was falling to pieces it was my own—I didn't go here, there and everywhere to find a place to kip for the night. So what was I always getting so irritated about? Why was I so desperate

還要什麼呢？不錯，真不錯。你怎麼樣？」他透過煙霧問我。我也感歎了，說：「錢是不少，糧也多，沒錯兒，可沒油哇。大鍋菜吃得胃酸。主要是沒什麼玩兒的，沒書，沒電，沒電影兒。去哪兒也不容易，老在這個溝兒裏轉，悶得無聊。」

他看看我，搖一下頭，說：「你們這些人哪！沒法兒說，想的淨是錦上添花。我挺知足，還要什麼呢？你呀，你就是叫書害了。你在車上給我講的兩個故事，我琢磨了，後來挺喜歡的。你不錯，讀了不少書。可是，歸到底，解決什麼呢？是呀？一個人拚命想活着，最後都神經了，後來好了，活下來了，可接着怎麼活呢？像邦斯那樣？有吃，有喝，好收藏個什麼，可有個饞的毛病，人家不請吃就活得不痛快。人要知足，頓頓飽就是福。」他不說了，看着自己的腳趾動來動去，又用後腳跟去擦另一隻腳的背，吐出一口煙，用手在腿上揮了揮。

我很後悔用油來表示我對生活的不滿意，還用書和電影兒這種可有可無的東西表示我對生活的不滿足，因為這些在他看來，實在是超出基準線之上的東西，他不會為這些煩悶。我突然覺得很泄氣，有些同意他的說法。是呀，還要什麼呢？我不是也感到挺好了嗎？不用吃了上頓惦記着下頓，牀不管怎麼爛，也還是自己的，不用竄來竄去找刷夜的地方。可我常常煩悶的是什麼呢？為什麼就那

to read a book, any old book? As for films, once the lights went up again the dream was over: what did I think I could get from them? But I still had a vague longing in my heart. I could not have said exactly what it was, but I realised that it was something to do with living.

"Do you still play chess?" I asked. "Of course," he replied, as quickly as he made a chess move. "Goes without saying." "Well then," I said, "if you think everything's so wonderful why do you still want to play chess? Isn't chess superfluous?" His smoke ring stopped in mid-air, he rubbed his face, and said, "I'm hooked on chess. Once I start playing I forget about everything else. As long as I'm lost in chess I'm happy. When I haven't got a board or pieces I can play it in my head. It's no skin off anyone's nose." "How would you feel if one day you weren't allowed to play chess, or even to think about it?" I asked. He looked at me with astonishment. "That's impossible. It couldn't happen. I could play in my head. They can't dig their way in there. You're talking nonsense." "Chess must be terrific," I sighed. "Once you've read a book you can't always be re-reading it in your head. You always want to read new ones. But chess isn't the same. You can change the games as you play them." "Well then," he said with a smile, "so you want to learn how to play chess? We've got no worries about having enough to eat—at worst it's not good enough—and life's pretty boring. There's nowhere you can get books, so play chess. Chess will ease your melancholy."

I thought it over, then said, "I'm really not interested in chess. But one of the chaps in our brigade is supposed to be good at it." He threw his cigarette end hard out of the door, and his eyes lit up again. "Really? A chess player? So I came to the right place. Where is he ?" "Not back from work yet," I replied. "What are you in such a rush for. Didn't you come to see me?" He lay on my bed with both hands behind his neck gazing at his slack belly. "It's six months since I've been able to find a chess player. Later on I thought that as the world is full of

麼想看看隨便什麼一本書呢？電影兒這種東西，燈一亮就全醒過來了，圖個什麼呢？可我隱隱有一種慾望在心裏，説不清楚，但我大致覺出是關於活着的什麼東西。

我問他：「你還下棋嗎？」他就像走棋那麼快地説：「當然，還用説？」我説：「是呀，你覺得一切都好，幹嗎還要下棋呢？下棋不多餘嗎？」他把煙卷兒停在半空，摸了一下臉，説：「我迷象棋。一下棋，就什麼都忘了。呆在棋裏舒服。就是沒有棋盤、棋子兒，我在心裏就能下，礙誰的事兒啦？」我説：「假如有一天不讓你下棋，也不許你想走棋的事兒，你覺得怎麼樣？」他挺奇怪地看着我説：「不可能，那怎麼可能？我能在心裏下呀！還能把我腦子挖了？你淨説些不可能的事兒。」我歎了一口氣，説：「下棋這事兒看來是不錯。看了一本兒書，你不能老在腦子裏過篇兒，老想看看新的。可棋不一樣了，自己能變着花樣兒玩。」他笑着對我説：「怎麼樣，學棋吧？咱們現在吃喝不愁了，頂多是照你説的，不夠好，又活不出個大意思來。書你哪兒找去？下棋吧，有憂下棋解。」

我想了想，説：「我實在對棋不感興趣。我們隊倒有個人，據説下得不錯。」他把煙屁股使勁兒扔出門外，眼睛又放出來光來：「真的？有下棋的？嘿，我真還來對了。他在哪兒？」我説：「還沒下班呢。看你急的，你不是來看我的嗎？」他雙手抱着脖子仰在我的被子上，看着自己鬆鬆的肚皮，説：「我這半年，就找不到下棋的。後來

remarkable people even in the backwoods here I'd surely be able to find a good chess player. I've taken some leave and been hunting for people to play chess with all along the way. Now I've got to your place."

"But you're not earning anything, are you?" I said. "What are you living on?" "You wouldn't know," he replied. "My sister's been given a job in industry in a city. As she's earning I don't have to send as much money home, so I thought I'd use this time to meet some chess players. What about it then? In a minute will you find that man you told me about to give me a game?" I said that of course I would, then with a quickening of my heart I asked another question, "What are things like at home?" He sighed and gazed at the ceiling. It was a long time before he said. "We're poor. It's very tough. There are three of us. My mother's dead. There's just my father, my kid sister and me. My dad earns next to nothing. If you average out what we've got to live on it's less than ten *yuan* each a month. My father's been drinking since my mother died, and it's been getting worse and worse. If he gets his hands on a bit of money he drinks and gets abusive. When the neighbours try to calm him down he's all too ready to listen. It's really embarrassing—he's all tears and snot. Once I asked him. 'Wouldn't you be better off not drinking? What good's it doing you?' 'You don't know what drink is,' he said to me. 'It's instead of sleep for us old men. We have a very hard life, your mother's gone, and you two are still young. I'm fed up. I've got no education and I'm getting on. The money I'm earning now will be all I'll ever have. When your mother died she said something about how I'd got to keep you till you'd finished junior middle school before letting you earn your living. Please let me have my drink. If you have grievances with your old man, let me pay for it in my next life.'"

Maniac gave me a look and then he said, "I'll tell you the truth. My mother was on the game before Liberation. After a while someone

想，天下異人多得很，這野林子裏我就不信找不到個下棋下得好的。現在我請了事假，一路找人下棋，就找到你這兒來了。」

我說：「你不掙錢了？怎麼活着呢？」他說：「你不知道，我妹妹在城裏分了工礦，掙錢啦，我也就不用給家寄那麼多錢了。我就想，趁這工夫兒，會會棋手。怎麼樣？你一會兒把你說的那人找來下一盤？」我說當然，心裏一動，就又問他：「你家裏到底是怎麼個情況呢？」他歎了一口氣，望着屋頂，很久才說：「窮。困難啊！我們家三口兒人，母親死了，只有父親、妹妹和我。我父親嘛，掙得少，按平均生活費的說法兒，我們一人才不到十塊。我母親死後，父親就喝酒，而且越喝越多，手裏有倆錢兒就喝，就罵人。鄰居勸，他不是不聽，就是一把鼻涕一把淚，弄得人家也挺難過。我有一回跟我父親說：『你不喝就不行？有什麼好處呢？』他說：『你不知道酒是什麼玩意兒，它是老爺們兒的覺啊！咱們這日子挺不易，你媽去了，你們又小。我煩哪，我沒文化，這把年紀，一輩子這點子錢算是到頭兒了。你媽死的時候，囑咐了，怎麼着也要供你唸完初中再掙錢。你們讓我喝口酒，啊？對老人有什麼過不去的，下輩子算吧。』」

他看了看我，又說：「不瞞你說，我母親解放前是窯子裏的。後

took a fancy to her and she became his concubine. So you could say that made her respectable. Can you give me a cigarette?" I threw him one, he lit it, blew on it till it was glowing red, and stared at it. His eyes didn't move. After a long time he said, "Later on my mother ran off with someone else. They say the man who'd bought her treated her badly, and it goes without saying what the senior wife did. They beat her too. I don't know what sort of bloke it was she went off with. All I know is that my mother started me with him. He disappeared straight after Liberation, leaving her pregnant with me. She had nothing to eat and nothing to wear, so she took up with my present father. He used to do heavy labour, but by the time Liberation came his strength gave out, and what with being uneducated he earned very little. Once he'd got together with my mum they hoped that they'd help each other to live a bit better, but after she had my sister my mother's health went from bad to worse. I'd just started at primary school. I had a good brain, and the teachers liked me. But I could never go on the school spring outings or trips to the cinema. I had to save everything I possibly could for the family. My mother didn't want to fail me, so although she was ill she dragged herself all over the place to find work. Once she and I were folding printed sheets for a printing shop. It was a book about chess. When we'd finished I checked them through, a book at a time. To my surprise I found it quite interesting.

"After that I went out to watch people playing chess in the streets whenever I had any spare time. And when I'd done that for a few days I started getting the itch. I didn't dare ask for any money, so I cut some pieces out of cardboard and took them to school. As I played I got used to the game. Then I went out to play on the street with other people. I could play very well when I was watching them, but when I started playing for real I lost. I played all evening. I didn't even eat. My mother came looking for me and hit me all the way home. She was so weak she couldn't even hurt me.

來大概是有人看上了，做了人家的小，也算從良。有煙嗎？」我扔過一根煙給他，他點上了，把煙頭兒吹得紅紅的，兩眼不錯眼珠兒地盯着，許久才說：「後來，我媽又跟人跑了。據說買她的那家欺負她，當老媽子不說，還打。後來跟的這個是什麼人，我不知道，我只知道我是我媽跟這個人生的，剛一解放，我媽跟的那個人就不見了。當時我媽懷着我，吃穿無着，就跟了我現在這個父親。我這個後爹是賣力氣的。可臨到解放的時候兒，身子骨兒不行了，又沒文化，錢就掙得少。和我媽過了以後，原指着相幫着好一點兒，可沒想到添了我妹妹後，我媽一天不如一天。那時候我才上小學，腦筋好，老師都喜歡我。可學校春遊、看電影我都不去，給家裏省一點兒是一點兒。我媽怕委屈了我，拖累着個身子，到處找活。有一回，我和我母親給印刷廠疊書頁子，是一本講象棋的書。疊好了，我媽還沒送去，我說一篇一篇對着看。不承想，就看出點兒意思來。

「於是有空兒就到街上看人家下棋。看了有些日子，就手癢癢，沒敢跟家裏要錢，自己用硬紙剪了一副棋，拿到學校去下。下着下着就熟了。於是又到街上和別人下。原先我看人家下得挺好，可我這一跟他們真下，還就贏了。一傢伙就下了一晚上，飯也沒吃。我媽找了來，把我打回去。唉，我媽身子弱，都打不疼我。

"When we got home she knelt down in front of me and said, 'Little ancestor, you're all my hopes. If you won't study properly I'm going to die here and now.' That gave me a terrible fright. 'Mum,' I said straight away, 'I've been studying properly. Please get up. I won't play chess any more.' I helped her up and into a chair. That night my mother and I were folding sheets, and as I went on and on folding my mind wandered off into a game of chess. 'Just look at you,' she said with a sigh. 'You can never afford to go to the cinema or a park. Play your chess. Go on then. But remember what I say: you mustn't go mad about playing. I won't forgive you if you mess up your lessons. Your dad and I can't read, but we can ask your teachers. If they say that you're not keeping up with your classes it won't matter what excuses you make.' I accepted that. I wasn't going to mess up my classes. School maths was like a game.

"From then on I'd do my home work after school then play chess. After supper I helped my mum with her work till bedtime. You don't have to use your brains to fold paper, so I could play chess in my head. Sometimes I got so carried away that I hit the pile of paper and shouted out a move. It gave them all a scare." "No wonder you play so well," I said. "You've had chess on the brain since you were a kid." "Yes," he smiled bitterly. "Later on the teacher urged me to join the chess group in the children's palace. They told me to learn as much as I could so I could be a champion later. But my mother said, 'We're not going to any chess group. If you want to study, learn a useful skill. However well you play chess you'll never be able to make a living from it. If you've got some spare time it'd be best to learn more at your school. Tell your teacher you're not going to the chess group. If there are things your teachers haven't taught you yet you tell them to teach you. It'll all come in very useful one day. What? You just want to learn chess? That used to be a game for the rich. I saw people like that in the old days. They were all somebody. They didn't play for their living.

「到了家，她竟給我跪下了，説：『小祖宗，我就指望你了！你若不好好兒唸書，媽就死在這兒。』我一聽這話嚇壞了，忙説：『媽，我沒不好好兒唸書。您起來，我不下棋了。』我把我媽扶起來坐着。那天晚上，我跟我媽疊頁子，疊着疊着，就走了神兒，想着一路棋。我媽歎一口氣説：『你也是，看不上電影兒，也不去公園，就玩兒這麼個棋。唉，下吧。可媽的話你得記着，不許玩兒瘋了。功課要是落下了，我不饒你。我和你爹都不識字兒，可我們會問老師。老師若説你功課跟不上，你再説什麼也不行。』我答應了。我怎麼會把功課落下呢？學校的算術，我跟玩兒似的。

「這以後，我放了學，先做功課，完了就下棋，吃完飯，就幫我媽幹活兒，一直到睡覺。因為疊頁子不用動腦筋，所以就在腦子裏走棋，有的時候，魔症了，會突然一拍書頁，喊棋步，把家裏人都嚇一跳。」我説：「怨不得你棋下得這麼好，小時候棋就都在你腦子裏呢！」他苦笑笑説：「是呀，後來老師就讓我去少年宮象棋組，説好好兒學，將來能拿大冠軍呢！可我媽説：『咱們不去什麼象棋組，要學，就學有用的本事。下棋下得好，還當飯吃了？有那點兒工夫，在學校多學點兒東西比什麼不好？你跟你們老師説，不去象棋組，要是你們老師還有沒教你的本事，你就跟老師説，你教了我，將來有大用呢。啊？專學下棋？這以前都是有錢人幹的！媽以前見

In the places where I used to live there were women who could play chess too—they charged more. You don't know. You don't understand. Playing for fun's all right, but don't specialise in it.'

"I told the teacher. He thought for a while but didn't say anything. Later on he bought me a chess set. When I showed it to my mum she said, 'What a kind man. But you remember, you've got to be able to earn your living first. Chess only comes second. When you're earning and supporting the family you can play as much as you like. It'll be up to you.'" I sighed and said, "So it's okay now. You're earning money, so you can play to your heart's content. Your mother needn't worry any more."

Wang Yisheng lifted his feet up on the bed and sat there cross-legged, his hands round his wrists, staring at the floor. "My mother never lived to see me earn anything," he continued. "My parents supported me till the first year of middle school, then she died. Before she died she said to me specially, 'Everyone in the street says you're good at chess. I believe them. But I don't like you for that. Chess'll get you nowhere. It's no living. I won't live to see you finish junior middle school, but I've told your father that he's got to see you through it no matter how hard up you are. From what I've heard, senior school is just for getting ready for university. In your family we don't need to go to university. Your dad's in a bad way and your sister's still a child. When you've finished junior middle school you can start earning. The family will depend on you. I'm leaving you now. I've not got anything to give you except this chess set I've made from old toothbrush handles I've picked up.' She told me to get a little cloth bundle out from under her pillow. When I opened it I found a set of tiny chessmen, polished as bright as ivory. But they didn't have their names written on them. 'As I can't read I was worried I'd carve the words wrong,' she said. 'Take them, and carve them yourself. That'll show you that your mum understands how much you like playing chess.' I'd never cried about

過這種人，那都有身份，他們不指着下棋吃飯。媽以前呆過的地方，也有女的會下棋，可要的錢也多。唉，你不知道，你不懂。下下玩兒可以，別專學，啊？』

我跟老師說了，老師想了想，沒說什麼。後來老師買了一副棋送我，我拿給媽看，媽說：『唉，這是善心人哪！可你記住，先說吃，再說下棋。等你掙了錢，養活家了，愛怎麼下就怎麼下，隨你。』我感歎了，說：「這下兒好了，你掙錢了，你就能撒着歡兒地下了，你媽也就放心了。」

王一生把腳搬上牀，盤了坐，兩隻手互相捏着腕子，看着地下說：「我媽看不見我掙錢了。家裏供我唸到初一，我媽就死了。死之前，特別跟我說：『這一條街都說你棋下得好，媽信，可媽在棋上疼不了你。你在棋上怎麼出息，到底不是飯碗。媽不能看你唸完初中，跟你爹說了，怎麼着困難，也要唸完。高中，媽打聽了，那是為上大學，咱們家用不着上大學，你爹也不行了，你妹妹還小，等你初中唸完了就掙錢，家裏就靠你了。媽要走了，一輩子也沒給你留下什麼，只撿人家的牙刷把，給你磨了一副棋。』說着，就叫我從枕頭底下拿出一個小布包來，打開一看，都是一小點兒大的子兒，磨得是光了又光，賽象牙，可上頭沒字兒。媽說，『我不識字，怕刻不對。你拿了去，自己刻吧，也算媽疼你好下棋。』我們家多困難，

any of our family's other troubles—what use would that have been—but when I saw that set of blank chessmen I couldn't help crying."

I felt a lump in my own throat, so I looked down and sighed. "What is it to be a mother ..." Wang Yisheng said nothing else, but just carried on smoking.

The others came down from the mountain with two snakes they had killed. When they saw Wang Yisheng they were all very polite, asking him which branch farm he was from and what the food was like there. He answered these questions then went to feel his clothes that had been hung out. They were not yet dry. I urged him to wear some of mine till they were ready, but he said he'd stay bare-chested for the time being as eating would make him sweat.

Seeing how easy-going he was everyone started talking casually. I naturally gave his chess playing a plug to let them know that he was no ordinary visitor, and they all said we ought to get the brigade's champion Legballs to come and give him a game. Someone went over to fetch him, and he was with us in no time.

Legballs was a school leaver from a big city in the south, very tall and very skinny. He moved in a rather refined way, and he was always very correctly dressed. To see someone like him, tall, elegant and beautifully burned out, when you were walking along a mountain path was really surprising. Legballs stooped to come in and stretched his hand out to shake when he was still some way off.

After a moment's confusion Wang Yisheng quickly realised who the newcomer was and stretched his hand out too. He blushed. After shaking hands Legballs clasped his hands in front of his stomach and said, "I'm called Ni Bin. As my legs are so long everyone calls me

我沒哭過，哭管什麼呢？可看着這副沒字兒的棋，我繃不住了。」

我鼻子有些酸，就低了眼，歎道：「唉，當母親的。」王一生不再說話，只是抽煙。

山上的人下來了，打到兩條蛇。大家見了王一生，都很客氣，問是幾分場的，那邊兒伙食怎麼樣。王一生答了，就過去摸一摸晾着的衣褲，還沒有乾。我讓他先穿我的，他說吃飯要出汗，先光着吧。大家見他很隨和，也就隨便聊起來。

我自然將王一生的棋道吹了一番，以示來者不凡。大家就都說讓隊裏的高手「腳卵」來與王一生下。一個人跑去喊，不一刻，腳卵來了，腳卵是南方大城市的知識青年，個子非常高，又非常瘦。動作起來頗有些文氣，衣服總要穿得整整齊齊，有時候走在山間小路上，看到這樣一個高個兒纖塵不染，衣冠楚楚，真令人生疑。腳卵彎腰進來，很遠就伸出手來要握。

王一生糊塗了一下，馬上明白了，也伸出手去，臉卻紅了。握過手，腳卵把雙手捏在一起端在肚子前面，說：「我叫倪斌，人兒倪，文武斌。因為腿長，大家叫我腳卵。卵是很粗俗的話，請不要

Legballs. 'Balls' is a crude word—I hope you won't mind. The people here are very uneducated. May I ask you name?" "Wang," he replied, looking up at Ni Bin who was a couple of heads taller than him, "Wang Yisheng."

"Wang Yisheng?" said Ni Bin. "Terrific, terrific, a terrific name. How do you write Yisheng?" Still looked up at him, Wang Yisheng told him. "Terrific, terrific," said Ni Bin, and he waved his long bent arm to add, "Do sit down. I hear that you've made a deep study of chess. Terrific, terrific. Chess represents a very high degree of culture. My father plays very well. He's quite well known. But they all know about that. I can play a bit and I'm very fond of it, but there's nobody to play with here. Do sit down."

Wang Yisheng went back to the bed and sat on it again, smiling awkwardly. He was at a loss for words. Ni Bin did not sit down himself, but put his hand on his chest, gave a slight bow and said, "I'm terribly sorry, but as I've just finished work I've not yet had time for a wash. Would you mind waiting a moment? I'll be right back. Oh, by the way, is your father a chess lover?" Wang Yisheng shook his head quickly and was on the point of saying something but only gasped instead. "Terrific, terrific," Ni Bin said. "Right then, I'll be back in a moment." "Legballs," I said, "come and have some snake after your bath." "There's no need," Ni Bin said as he left, "no need. All right then, all right." Everyone burst out laughing. "Are you coming or aren't you?" they shouted after him. "What do you mean, 'no need, all right then'?" "Of course I want to eat snake," Ni Bin said from the other side of the door. "I'll have to use my head when I play chess in a moment."

As they all laughed at Legballs they shut the door, stripped naked, and washed themselves all over, teasing each other about their bodies. Goodness knows what Wang Yisheng was thinking about as he sat on

介意，這裏的人文化水平是很低的。貴姓？」王一生比倪斌矮下去兩個頭，就仰着頭說：「我姓王，叫王一生。」

倪斌說：「王一生？蠻好，蠻好，名字蠻好的。一生是哪兩個字？」王一生一直仰着脖子，說：「一二三的一，生活的生。」倪斌說：「蠻好，蠻好。」就把長臂曲着往外一擺，說：「請坐。聽說你鑽研象棋？蠻好，蠻好，象棋是很高級的文化。我父親是下得很好的，有些名氣，喏，他們都知道的。我會走一點點，很愛好，不過在這裏沒有對手。你請坐。」

王一生坐回牀上，很尷尬地笑着，不知說什麼好。倪斌並不坐下，只把手虛放在胸前，微微向前側了一下身子，說：「對不起，我剛剛下班，還沒有梳洗，你候一下好了，我馬上就來。噢，問一下，乃父也是棋道裏的人麼？」王一生很快地搖頭，剛要說什麼，但只是喘了一口氣。倪斌說：「蠻好，蠻好。一會兒我再來。」我說：「腳卵洗了澡，來吃蛇肉。」倪斌一邊退出去，一邊說：「不必了，好的。」大家笑起來，向外嚷：「你到底來不來？什麼『不必了，不必了。』好的，好的。」倪斌在門外說：「蛇肉當然是要吃的，一會兒下棋是要動腦筋的。」

大家笑着腳卵，關了門，三四個人精着屁股，上上下下地洗，互相開着身體的玩笑。王一生不知在想什麼，坐在牀裏邊，讓開擦

the edge of the bed, keeping out of the way of the men towelling themselves. I ripped the heads off the snakes and said to him, "Never mind about Legballs. He's just crazy." "If this pal of yours really knows his stuff we'll have a good game today," one of the lads said to me. "Legballs' dad's famous in our city." "The father's one thing and the son's another," put in someone else. "Chess playing isn't a hereditary skill." "Some very good players have learnt their chess at home," said Wang Yisheng. "Games that have been kept in a family for generations can't be underestimated. We'll see when we start playing." As he spoke his hands and face tensed up.

I hung up the snakes and skinned them but did not wash them, then put them on the table and opened them up with a bamboo knife. Instead of cutting them up I coiled them up in a big bowl that I stood in a pot. Then I put water in the bottom of the pot and called out, "Have you finished washing yet? I'm going to open the door." They scrambled into their undershorts. I went out and made a stand with three sun-dried bricks, piled some kindling between them and stood the pot on the bricks, shouting at the pigs to keep them away. "Who's going to watch this?" I asked. "Don't let the pigs knock it over. Take it off the heat ten minutes after it's started boiling." I went back inside to prepare the aubergines.

Someone washed a washing bowl clean and took it to the canteen to fetch four or five pounds of rice and a little bowl of plain boiled eggplants. He also brought back a scallion, two cloves of wild garlic and a small piece of ginger. When I said we were still short of salt someone else ran back to fetch a block of salt that was then smashed up and put on a sheet of paper.

Legballs made his long journey back with a black wooden box in his hands. "Have you got any condensed soy sauce, Legballs?" I asked. After a moment's hesitation he went back. "And bring us some vinegar crystals if you've got any," I shouted after him.

身的人。我一邊將蛇頭撕下來，一邊對王一生説：「別理腳卵，他就是這麼神神道道的一個人。」有一個人對我説：「你的這個朋友要真是有兩下子，今天有一場好殺。腳卵的父親在我們市裏，真是很有名氣哩。」另外的人説：「爹是爹，兒是兒，棋還遺傳了？」王一生説：「家傳的棋，有厲害的。幾代沉下的棋路，不可小看。一會兒下起來看吧。」説着就緊一緊手臉。

我把蛇掛起來，將皮剝下，不洗，放在案板上，用竹刀把肉劃開，並不切斷，盤在一個大碗內，放進一個大鍋裏，鍋底蓄上水，叫：「洗完了沒有？我可開門了！」大家慌忙穿上短褲。我到外邊地上擺三塊土坯，中間架起柴引着，就將鍋放在土坯上，把豬吆喝遠了，説：「誰來看看？別叫豬拱了。開鍋後十分鐘端下來。」就進屋收拾茄子。

有人把臉盆洗乾淨，到伙房打了四五斤飯和一小盆清水茄子，捎回來一棵蔥和兩瓣野蒜、一小塊薑，我説還缺鹽，就又有人跑去拿來一塊，搗碎在紙上放着。

腳卵遠遠地來了，手裏抓着一個黑木盒子。我問：「腳卵，可有醬油膏？」腳卵遲疑了一下，返身回去。我又大叫：「有醋精拿點兒來！」

When the snakes were cooked I carried them inside and whipped off the lid to let out a great cloud of steam. Instead of pulling their heads back they all waited till they could see the meat then exclaimed in admiration. The two snakes were coiled gleaming in the bowl, appetizing steam rising from them. I whisked the blowl out of the pot and blew my fingers as I said, "Get you digestive juices ready." Wang Yisheng pushed over too to take a look. "How can we eat them whole?" he asked. "Snake meat mustn't come into contact with iron," I said. "If it does it stinks. That's why I didn't cut it up. Tear it apart with your chopsticks, dip it in the flavourings, and eat it." I put the sliced eggplant into the pot to steam.

Legballs came in with a small piece of condensed soy sauce wrapped in paper and another little paper packet in which were a few white crystals. When I asked him what they were he said, "It's oxalic acid. It's meant to be used as disinfectant, but you can use it instead of vinegar. I have't got any vinegar crystals, and this is all the concentrated soy I've got left." "We'll make do," I said. Legball put his box on the table and opened it. It was a chess set, and the dark, shiny pieces were made of ebony. The characters on each piece were archaic ones engraved with the most careful writing and inlaid in gold and silver wire. They had a very ancient and distinguished air to them. The board was made of silk instead of paper, and the writing on it was also archaic. Everyone crowded round to look at it, to Legballs' great satisfaction. "It's an antique," he said, "Ming dynasty, and very valuable. My father gave it to me when I came here. I didn't need a good set like this when I played with you before. But today, now that Wang Yisheng's here, we can play properly." Wang Yisheng, who had probably never seen so exquisite a chess set in his life, fondled the pieces very carefully and tensed up again.

　　蛇肉到了時間，端進屋裏，掀開鍋，一大團蒸汽冒出來，大家並不縮頭，慢慢看清了，都叫一聲好。兩大條蛇肉亮晶晶地盤在碗裏，粉粉地冒鮮氣。我嗖地一下將碗端出來，吹吹手指，説：「開始準備胃液吧！」王一生也擠過來看，問：「整着怎麼吃？」我説：「蛇肉碰不得鐵，碰鐵就腥，所以不切，用筷子撕着蘸料吃。」我又將切好的茄塊兒放進鍋裏蒸。

　　腳卵來了，用紙包了一小塊兒醬油膏，又用一張小紙包了幾顆白色的小粒兒，我問是什麼，腳卵説：「這是草酸，去污用的，不過可以代替醋。我沒有醋精，醬油膏也沒有了，就這一點點。」我説：「湊合了。」腳卵把盒子放在牀上，打開，原來是一副棋，烏木做的棋子，暗暗的發亮。字用刀刻出來，筆劃很細，卻是篆字，用金絲銀絲嵌了，古色古香。棋盤是一幅絹，中間亦是篆字：楚河漢界。大家湊過去看，腳卵就很得意，説：「這是古董，明朝的，很值錢。我來的時候，我父親給我的。以前和你們下棋，用不到這麼好的棋。今天王一生來嘛，我們好好下。」王一生大約從來沒有見過這麼精采的棋具，很小心地摸，又緊一緊手臉。

I poured water on the condensed soy and the oxalic acid crystals, added chopped up scallions and ginger, and shouted, "Eat!" They all noisily filled their bowls with rice, tore the snake meat apart with their chopsticks, dipped it into the sauce, and said how marvellous it was as soon as it was in their mouths.

I asked Wang Yisheng if he thought it was a bit like crab. "I've never had crab," he replied as he chewed, "so I can't tell." At this Legballs leaned over to ask, "Never eaten crab? How's that possible?" Wang Yisheng did not answer, but carried on eating. Legballs put his bowl and chopsticks down. "Every Mid-Autumn Festival," he said, "my father invites some of his famous friends to our home to eat crab, play chess, appreciate good wine, and write poems. They're all very cultured people and their poems are very good. They write them on fans for each other. The fans will be worth a lot many years from now." Everyone ignored him and carried on eating. Seeing that there was less and less of the snake left he snatched his chopsticks up again and stopped talking.

It was not long before the snake meat was all finished leaving only a couple of snake skeletons in the bowl. I then brought the steamed aubergine in and mixed garlic and salt in with it. Then I tipped the hot water out of the pot and replaced it with fresh, into which I put the snake bones for soup. Everyone gasped, stretched out their chopsticks again, and soon finished off the eggplant. I then brought the soup in. After boiling, the snake bones had all come apart and were rattling in the bottom of the pot. There were always a few clumps of wild aniseed growing outside the building, and when I picked a few and plunged them into the hot soup the room was immediately filled with a rich aroma. By now they had eaten all the rice, and as they ladled the soup into their bowls and slowly sipped it hot, they were more relaxed than before and their tongues loosened.

我將醬油膏和草酸沖好水，把蔥末、薑末和蒜末投進去，叫聲：「吃起來！」大家就乒乒乓乓地盛飯，伸筷撕那蛇肉蘸料，剛入嘴嚼，紛紛嚷鮮。

我問王一生是不是有些像蟹肉，王一生一邊兒嚼着，一邊兒說：「我沒吃過螃蟹，不知道。」腳卵伸過頭去問：「你沒吃過螃蟹？怎麼會呢？」王一生也不答話，只顧吃。腳卵就放下碗筷，說：「年年中秋節，我父親就約一些名人到家裏來，吃螃蟹，下棋，品酒，作詩。都是些很高雅的人，詩做得很好的，還要互相寫在扇子上。這些扇子過多少年也是很值錢的。」大家並不理會他，只顧吃。腳卵眼看蛇肉漸少，也急忙捏起筷子夾，不再說什麼。

不一刻，蛇肉吃完，只剩兩副蛇骨在碗裏。我又把蒸熟的茄塊兒端上來，放少許蒜和鹽拌了。再將鍋裏熱水倒掉，續上新水，把蛇骨放進去熬湯。大家喘一口氣，接着伸筷，不一刻，茄子也吃淨。我便把湯端上來，蛇骨已經煮散，在鍋底刷拉刷拉地響。這裏屋外常有一二處小叢的野茴香，我就拔來幾棵，揪在湯裏，立刻屋裏異香撲鼻。大家這時飯已吃淨，紛紛舀了湯在碗裏，熱熱的小口呷，不似剛才緊張，話也多起來了。

"Terrific, it's terrific," said Legballs, pushing his hat back. He brought out a cigarette that he gave to Wang Yisheng, then put another into his own mouth. He was just about to put the packet back in his pocket when he thought for a moment, placed it on a small table, waved his hands and said, "What we've eaten today have all been mountain delicacies. We haven't been able to get any seafood. We eat a lot of seafood in my family: we're really particular about it. My father told me that when my grandfather was alive he used to employ an old woman who spent all day removing the dirt from birds' nests. These birds' nests are made by a kind of sea bird from little fish and shrimps stuck together with its saliva, which is why there are so many mucky bits in them that have to be removed one by one and very carefully. You can only clean up one a day. Then you steam it very gently over a low fire. If you eat a bit every day it's very good for you."

"Blimey," said Wang Yisheng, "someone spending all her time just preparing birds' nests. Wouldn't it have been just as good as birds' nests to buy some fish and shrimps and boil them up together?"

"If you could, would birds' nests be so expensive?" said Legballs with a touch of a smile. "In the first place, the nests are built on cliffs by the ocean, and you have to risk your neck to get them. Second, the sea bird's saliva is very valuable: it's warming and strengthening. So birds' nests need risking someone's life, cost a lot of time and are a tonic. It shows your family is rich and you're really someone if you can eat them." Everyone then said that birds' nests must be very delicious. Legballs gave a little smile and said: "I've eaten them. They stink." Everybody sighed and said it wasn't worth spending so much to eat something high.

It grew dark. The moon that had risen some time before gradually became lighter. I lit an oil lamp that cast people's shadows on all the walls. "Shall we have a game, Wang Yisheng?" Legballs asked. Wang

腳卵抹一抹頭髮，說：「蠻好，蠻好的。」就拿出一支煙，先讓了王一生，又自己叼了一支，煙包正待放回衣袋裏，想了想，便放在小飯桌上，擺一擺手說：「今天吃的，都是山珍，海味是吃不到了。我家裏常吃海味的，非常講究。據我父親講，我爺爺在時，專雇一個老太婆，整天就是從燕窩裏撥髒東西。燕窩這種東西，是海鳥叼來小魚小蝦，用口水粘起來的。所以裏面各種髒東西多得很，要很細心地一點一點清理，一天也就能搞清一個，再用小火慢慢地蒸。每天吃一點，對身體非常好。」

王一生聽呆了，問：「一個人每天就專門是管做燕窩的？好家伙！自己買來魚蝦，熬在一起，不等於燕窩嗎？」

腳卵微微一笑，說：「要不怎麼燕窩貴呢？第一，這燕窩長在海中峭壁上，要捨命去挖。第二，這海鳥的口水是很珍貴的東西，是溫補的。因此，捨命，費工時，又是補品；能吃燕窩，也是說明家裏有錢和有身份。」大家就說這燕窩一定非常好吃。腳卵又微微一笑，說：「我吃過的，很腥。」大家就感歎了，說費這麼多錢，吃一口腥，太划不來。

天黑下來，早升在半空的月亮漸漸亮了。我點起油燈，立刻四壁都是人影子。腳卵就說：「王一生，我們下一盤？」王一生大

Yisheng probably had not yet woken up from his thoughts of birds' nests, as he only gave a slight nod in response. Legballs went outside, at which Wang Yisheng gave a grunt of surprise. There was general laughter but no explanation. A moment later Legballs came back inside, very correctly dressed, followed by many other people who all came in to have a look at Wang Yisheng. Legballs slowly set the pieces out. "Will you move first?" he asked. "You," said Wang Yisheng. Everyone gathered around, some sitting and some standing, to watch.

After a dozen or so moves Wang Yisheng was rather uneasy, but all he did was to quietly rub his fingers. When thirty or so moves had been made Wang Yisheng quickly said, "Let's have another game." Everyone looked with astonishment at Wang Yisheng then at Legballs: they did not know who had won. "One win doesn't constitute a victory," said Legballs with a smile, putting his hand out for a cigarette and lighting it. Wang Yisheng did not show his feelings as he set the pieces out again in silence. The two of them started playing again. After another dozen or so moves Legballs did nothing for a long time until he had finished his cigarette. They made a few more moves, then Legballs slowly said, "Let's have another game." Everyone wondered once more who had won and kept asking. Wang Yisheng quickly put the pieces into a square pile, looked at Legballs and said, "What about playing blind?" Legballs thought for a moment then nodded. Then two of them started calling out their moves. Quite a few of the spectators started scratching their heads and their necks and saying that this was a boring way of playing as you couldn't tell who was winning. Some of them left, taking some of the oil lamps with them and leaving the room half in darkness.

Feeling a little cold I asked Wang Yisheng, "Don't you want to put something on?" He ignored me. I felt bored too, so I sat down on the bed, looking first at the crowd, then at Legballs and at Wang Yisheng as if I were examining a couple of monsters for the first time. By the

概還沒有從燕窩裏醒過來，聽見腳卵問，只微微點一點頭。腳卵出去了。王一生奇怪了，問：「嗯？」大家笑而不答。一會兒，腳卵又來了，穿得筆挺，身後隨來許多人，進屋都看看王一生。腳卵慢慢擺好棋，問：「你先走？」王一生說：「你吧。」大家就上上下下圍了看。

走出十多步，王一生有些不安，但也只是暗暗捻一下手指。走過三十幾步，王一生很快地說：「重擺吧。」大家奇怪，看看王一生，又看看腳卵，不知是誰贏了。腳卵微微一笑，說：「一贏不算勝。」就伸手抽一顆煙點上。王一生沒有表情，默默地把棋重新碼好。兩人又走。又走到十多步，腳卵半天不動，直到把一根煙吸完，又走了幾步，腳卵慢慢地說：「再來一盤。」大家又奇是誰贏了，紛紛問。王一生很快地將棋碼成一個方堆，看着腳卵問：「走盲棋。」腳卵沉吟了一下，點點頭。兩人就口述棋步。好幾個人摸摸頭，摸摸脖子，說下得好沒意思，不知誰是贏家，就有幾個人離開走出去，把油燈帶得一明一暗。

我覺出有點兒冷，就問王一生：「你不穿點兒衣裳？」王一生沒有理我。我感到沒有意思，就坐在牀裏，看大家也是一會兒看看腳卵，一會兒看看王一生，像是瞧從來沒見過的兩個怪物。油燈下，

light of the paraffin lamp Wang Yisheng sat with his arms round his knees. There were two deep hollows behind his collarbones. He was staring at the lamp. Every now and then he hit a mosquito that landed on him. Legballs' long legs were against his chest. One large hand was covering the whole of his face while the finger of his other hand fidgetted rapidly. After they had been talking for a long time Legballs put his hands down, gave a quick smile, and said, "I'm muddled. I can't remember where I am." He set the pieces out for another game. It was not long before he looked up at Wang Yisheng and said, "The world is yours." He pulled out a cigarette and handed it to Wang Yisheng with the question, "Who taught you to play?" Wang Yisheng looked at Legballs and replied, "People everywhere." "Terrific, terrific," said Legballs. "You're a terrific player." Now that we all had seen who the winner was we all relaxed cheerfully and gazed at Wang Yisheng.

Lagballs rubbed his hands and said, "My chess has got rusty with no chess players here. I'm really pleased to have met you today. We're friends now." "I'll certainly go to see your father when I get the chance," said Wang Yisheng. "Good, great," said Legballs with delight. "You must go and see him when you can. I'm not a serious player." After a moment's pause he continued, "I'm sure you'll be able to get into the local tournament." "What tournament?" "We're having a sports meet in the district. There'll be chess and the like. I know the secretary in charge of education and culture for the district. He used to know my father in our home town. When I came to the state farm my father gave me a letter for him asking him to look after me. I went to see him, and he told me that I'd better play basketball. But how could I? It's such a savage game—you can get hurt. He wrote to tell me about this sports meet and get me to join our farm's board games team and go to the district meet. If I win, a transfer will of course be easy. A player like you would be bound to get into the farm team. All you have to do

王一生抱了雙膝，鎖骨後陷下兩個紳窩，盯着油燈，時不時拍一下
身上的蚊蟲。腳卵兩條長腿抵在胸口，一隻大手將整個兒臉遮了，
另一隻大手飛快地將指頭捏來弄去。說了許久，腳卵放下手，很快
地笑一笑，說：「我亂了，記不得。」就又擺了棋再下。不久，腳卵
抬起頭，看看王一生說：「天下是你的。」抽出一支煙給王一生，又
說：「你的棋是跟誰學的？」王一生也看着腳卵，說：「跟天下人。」
腳卵說：「蠻好，蠻好，你的棋蠻好。」大家看出是誰贏了，都高興
得鬆動起來，盯着王一生看。

　　腳卵把手搓來搓去，說：「我們這裏沒有會下棋的人，我的棋路
生了。今天碰到你，蠻高興的，我們做個朋友。」王一生說：「將來
有機會，一定見見你父親。」腳卵很高興，說：「那好，好極了，有
機會一定去見見他。我不過是玩玩棋。」停了一會兒，又說：「你參
加地區的比賽，沒有問題。」王一生問：「什麼比賽？」腳卵說：「咱
們地區，要組織一個運動會，其中有棋類。地區管文教的書記我認
得，他早年在我們市裏，與我父親認識。我到農場來，我父親給他
帶過信，請他照顧。我找過他，他說我不如打籃球。我怎麼會打籃
球呢？那是很野蠻的運動，要傷身體的。這次運動會，他來信告訴
我，讓我爭取參加農場的棋類隊到地區比賽，贏了，調動自然好
說。你棋下到這個地步，參加農場隊，不成問題。你回你們場，去

is come back to our farm and put down your name. When they have the trials at farm headquarters you're bound to be chosen." Wang Yisheng was delighted. He looked skinnier than ever when he got up to put some clothes on.

At almost midnight the party broke up, leaving only the four of us who lived in the same room, Wang Yisheng and Legballs. Legballs stood up and said, "I'm going to fetch something to eat." Everyone waited in high excitement until he bent low to come back in again and put his things on the bed. He displayed six bars of chocolate, half a packet of malted milk powder and a pound of best white noodles wrapped in paper. We all gulped down the chocolate and licked our lips. We added hot water to the malted milk powder and made up six very weak bowlfuls that we all drank noisily. "There can't be anything else like this in the world," said Wang Yisheng with a giggle. "It's bitter and sweet at the same time." I turned the stove up, brought water in the pan to the boil and put the noodles in. "Pity we've got nothing to flavour them with," I said. "I've got some more concentrated soy," said Legballs. "I thought you only had that little bit," I said. "Well," replied Legballs with embarrassment, "today's a special occasion as Wang Yisheng's here. I can contribute a bit more." He went off to fetch it.

When we'd all eaten we lit up, yawned and said we'd never have imagined that Legballs would have so much stashed away. He'd hidden his things really well. Legballs quickly explained that this really was everything he had left. When we all said we were going to search his place Wang Yisheng protested, "Don't fool around. What's his is his. If he's kept stuff from when he arrived at the farm right up till now that shows he's a good housekeeper. Tell me, Ni Bin, when does this tournament start?" "It's to be at least six months from now," Legballs replied. Wang Yisheng said nothing else. "All right," I said, "let's go to bed. Wang Yisheng, you can double up with me in my bed.

報名就可以了。將來總場選拔，肯定會有你。」王一生很高興，起來把衣裳穿上，顯得更瘦，大家又聊了很久。

將近午夜，大家都散去，只剩下宿舍裏同住的四個人與王一生、腳卵。腳卵站起來，說：「我去拿些東西來吃。」大家都很興奮，等着他。一會兒，腳卵彎腰進來，把東西放在牀上，擺出六顆巧克力，半袋麥乳精，紙包的一斤精白掛麵。巧克力大家都一口咽了，來回舐着嘴唇。麥乳精沖成稀稀的六碗，喝得滿屋喉嚨響。王一生笑嘻嘻地說：「世界上還有這種東西？苦甜苦甜的。」我又把火升起來，開了鍋，把麵下了，說：「可惜沒有調料。」腳卵說：「我還有醬油膏。」我說：「你不是只有一小塊兒了嗎？」腳卵不好意思地說：「咳，今天不容易，王一生來了，我再貢獻一些。」就又拿了來。

大家吃了，紛紛點起煙，打着哈欠，說沒想到腳卵還有如許存貨，藏得倒嚴實，腳卵急忙申辯這是剩下的全部了。大家吵着要去翻，王一生說：「不要鬧，人家的是人家的，從來農場存到現在，說明人家會過日子。倪斌，你說，這比賽什麼時候開始呢？」腳卵說：「起碼還有半年。」王一生不再說話。我說：「好了，休息吧。王一生，你和我睡在我的牀上。腳卵，明天再聊。」大家就起身收拾牀

We can go on talking tomorrow, Legballs." We all stood up to make the beds and put up the mosquito nets. Wang Yisheng and I escorted Legballs to the door and watched his tall shape vanish into the distance under the blue and white moonlight. Wang Yisheng sighed and said, "Ni Bin's a good bloke."

Wang Yisheng stayed for another day but insisted on going the morning after that. Legballs came in tattered old clothes and with his mattock over his shoulder to say goodbye. As the two of them shook hands Ni Bin said, "We'll definitely meet again." They all waved to Wang Yisheng from far up the mountainside. I went with him to the end of the little valley, where he stopped me and told me to go back. I insisted that if he got into difficulties at any of the other branches of the farm he was to get someone to bring me a message, and that if he came this way on his journey back he was to come and spend some more time with us. Wang Yisheng adjusted the strap of his satchel and hurried off along the highway, raising the dust with his feet, his clothes waving. His trousers flapped about as if he had no backside inside them.

舖，放蚊帳。我和王一生送腳卵到門口，看他高高的個子在青白的月光下遠遠去了。王一生歎一口氣，説：「倪斌是個好人。」

王一生又呆了一天，第三天早上，執意要走。腳卵穿了破衣服，揹着鋤來送。兩人握了手，倪斌説：「後會有期。」大家遠遠在山坡上招手。我送王一生出了山溝，王一生攔住，説：「回去吧。」我囑咐他，到了別的分場，有什麼困難，託人來告訴我，若回來路過，再來玩兒。王一生整了整書包帶兒，就急急地順公路走了，腳下揚起細土，衣裳晃來晃去，褲管兒前後蕩着，像是沒有屁股。

3

From then on we often talked about Wang Yisheng when we were at a loose end, relishing the memory of his bare-shouldered battle with Legballs. When I told them what a hard life Wang Yisheng had had Legballs said, "My father says that 'great scholars come from poor families'. He told me that Ni Yunlin of the Yuan dynasty was our ancestor, and he liked having everything clean. At first the family was rich, so he could have everything just so. After that we were ruined by the wars, so our ancestor sold the family property and wandered all over the place. He often slept in villages and inns in the back of nowhere and met a lot of great scholars. Later on he got to know some people living in the wilds who could play chess, and they taught him to play really well. Nowadays everyone's heard of Ni Yunlin the great poet, calligrapher and painter who was one of the four masters of the Yuan period. They don't realise he was a chess player too. Later on he became a Zen Buddhist and brought chess into the Zen tradition. He developed his own school of chess that was only handed down in our family. I don't know what school Wang Yisheng belongs to, but he beat me and he's certainly a very good player." None of us knew who Ni Yunlin was, and we only half believed Legballs' boasting. But we accepted that Legballs knew a thing or two about chess, and that as Wang Yisheng had beaten Legballs he must be even greater. All the other educated youngsters there came from the common people of the cities, and most of them were from poor families, which made them appreciate Wang Yisheng even more.

這以後，大家沒事兒，常提起王一生，津津有味兒地回憶王一生光膀子大戰腳卵。我說了王一生如何如何不容易，腳卵說：「我父親說過的，『寒門出高士』。據我父親講，我們祖上是元朝的倪雲林。倪祖很愛乾淨，開始的時候，家裏有錢，當然是講究的。後來兵荒馬亂，家道敗了，倪祖就賣了家產，到處走，常在荒村野店投宿，很遇到一些高士。後來與一個會下棋的村野之人相識，學得一手好棋。現在大家只曉得倪雲林是元四家裏的一個，詩書畫絕佳，卻不曉得倪雲林還會下棋。倪祖後來信佛參禪，將棋煉進禪宗，自成一路。這棋只我們這一宗傳下來。王一生贏了我，不曉得他是什麼路，總歸是高手了。」大家都不知道倪雲林是什麼人，只聽腳卵神吹，將信將疑，可也認定腳卵的棋有些來路，王一生既贏了腳卵，當然更了不起。這裏的知青在城裏都是平民出身，多是寒苦的，自然更看重王一生。

Nearly six months passed, but we saw no more of Wang Yisheng. All we got were reports from here and there that someone called Wang Yisheng whose nickname was the Chess Maniac had played chess with someone or other at some place or other and beaten him. We were all delighted, and even when there was news of his being beaten we always refused to believe it: how could Wang Yisheng possibly lose? When there was no answer to the letter I wrote to him at his branch farm the others all urged me to go and see him. But what with one thing and another, and on top of everything else the frequent feuds between the young school-leavers in the farms, and the shooting at each other with firearms that had been brought in, I did not go in the end.

One day on the mountainside Legballs told me that he had put his name down for the chess tournament and would be going to farm headquarters in a couple of days' time. He asked me if I'd had any news of Wang Yisheng. I said that I had not. We all said that Wang Yisheng was bound to go to farm headquarters for the chess tournament and we agreed that we would all ask for leave to go to headquarters to watch.

A couple of days later the work in the brigade slackened off and the others all asked for leave to go to headquarters on various pretexts in the hope of seeing Wang Yisheng. I asked for leave too and went with them.

The farm headquarters was in the district capital, and it took us two days to get there. Although the place was an administrative centre at the level immediately below the province all it had were two streets that crossed each other with some shops in them. The shelves in the shops were either empty of full of "Display Goods: Not for Sale". But we were still excited, and felt that we had come to somewhere prosperous and splendid. We ate our way from one inn to the next along the street. We called for plain boiled pork and wolfed dish after

　　將近半年，王一生不再露面。只是這裏那裏傳來消息，說有個叫王一生的，外號棋呆子，在某處與某某下棋，贏了某某。大家也很高興，即使有輸的消息，都一致否認，說王一生怎麼會輸呢？我給王一生所在的分場隊裏寫了信，也不見回音，大家就催我去一趟。我因為這樣那樣的事，加上農場知青常常鬥毆，又輸進火藥槍互相射擊，路途險惡，終於沒有去。

　　一天腳卵在山上對我說，他已經報名參加棋類比賽了，過兩天就去總場，問王一生可有消息？我說沒有。大家就說王一生肯定會到總場比賽，相約一起請假去總場看看。

　　過了兩天，隊裏的活兒稀鬆，大家就紛紛找了各種藉口請假到總場，盼着能見着王一生。我也請了假出來。

　　總場就在地區所在地，大家走了兩天才到。這個地區雖是省以下的行政單位，卻只有交叉的兩條街，沿街有一些商店，貨架上不是空的，即是「展品概不出售」。可是大家仍然很興奮，覺得到了繁華地界，就沿街一個館子一個館子地吃，都先只叫淨肉，一盤一盤地吞下去，拍拍肚子出來，覺得日光晃眼，竟有些肉醉，就找了一處草

dish of it, then we patted our bellies and found the sunlight rather dazzling. We were rather drunk with meat, so we found some grass on which to stretch out. We smoked then went to sleep. When we woke up we went back to the shopping streets to eat some grain-based food with deliberate relish, then went to the farm headquarters.

A whole column of us went to the headquarters in the highest of spirits, where we found an official who dealt with education and sport and asked whether someone by the name of Wang Yisheng had reported in. The official spent a long time checking the register then told us that he had not. We did not believe him, so we grabbed the register and all snatched at it as we looked through it, only to find that his name really was not there. We asked the official if Wang Yisheng could have been left out by mistake, and the official said that the register had been compiled from the names the branch farms submitted. Everyone had been given a number and assigned to a group. The games would begin the next day. We all looked at each other in bewilderment. "Let's go and find Legballs," I suggested. He was in the thatched huts where the athletes were staying, and as soon as we saw him we asked him. "I can't understand it either," he said. "It's chaos here. I've been given a number as a chess player, but they've put me to stay with the ball players. They insist that I've got to take part in this evening's training session for the headquarters team. I argued for ages but it was no use at all. They said they'd be depending on me to get the ball forward." We all burst out laughing and said, "Never mind what kind of competition it is: you'll be eating well enough. But it's a real pity that Wang Yisheng's not here."

Even when the games began there was still no sign of Wang Yisheng. When we asked some people from his branch farm they all said that they had not seen him for ages. We were worried, but there was nothing we could do, so we went to watch Legballs playing basketball. He was having a thoroughly miserable time. He knew none

地，躺下來抽煙，又紛紛昏睡過去。醒來後，大家又回到街上細細吃了一些麵食，然後到總場去。

一行人高高興興到了總場，找到文體幹事，問可有一個叫王一生的來報到。幹事翻了半天花名冊，說沒有。大家不信，拿過花名冊來七手八腳地找，真的沒有，就問幹事是不是搞漏掉了。幹事說花名冊是按各分場報上來的名字編的，都已分好號碼，編好組，只等明天開賽。大家你望望我，我望望你，搞不清是怎麼回事兒。我說：「找腳卵去。」腳卵在運動員們住下的草棚裏，見了他，大家就問。腳卵說：「我也奇怪呢。這裏亂糟糟的，我的號是棋類，可把我分到球類組來住，讓我今晚就參加總場聯隊訓練，說了半天也不行，還說主要靠我進球得分。」大家笑起來，說：「管他賽什麼，你們的伙食差不了。可王一生沒來太可惜了。」

直到比賽開始，也沒有見王一生的影子。問了他們分場來的人，都說很久沒見王一生了。大家有些慌，又沒辦法，只好去看腳卵賽籃球。腳卵痛苦不堪，規矩一點兒不懂，球也抓不住，投出去

of the rules, could not even hold on to the ball properly, and missed every time he threw. Whenever there was a scramble for the ball that got at all fierce he removed himself and watched wide-eyed while the rest of them struggled. The official in charge of culture and sport was scratching his ears in despair and everyone else was rocking about with laughter. Every time he came off Legballs yelled and complained about how barbaric and filthy it all was.

After two days of trials all the farm headquarters teams were chosen for the games. When we saw that there was still no sign of Wang Yisheng we all agreed that we would go back. Legballs wanted to stay with the district secretary for culture and education for another couple of days, and he saw us off on the beginning of our journey. We had almost reached the crossroads when someone pointed and said, "Isn't that Wang Yisheng?" We looked that way and saw that it really was him. Wang Yisheng was rushing towards the corner and had not noticed us. When we all called out to him he came to a violent halt, saw us, and crossed the road towards us. As he came close we all asked at once why he had not come to take part in the tournament. He looked very anxious as he replied, "I've been taking leave to go off and play chess for the last six months, but when I knew it was time to put my name down and come back, the branch farm wouldn't let me come here for the tournament. They didn't even put my name forward. They said I'd been behaving too badly. I've only just found an excuse to come here and watch the tournament. How is it? How's the play been?" Everyone answered at once that the early rounds were over and that what was happening now was the competition between the county teams for the district championship.

Wang Yisheng was silent for a while. Then he said, "All right. It must be the best players from all the counties who are going in for the district championship. It'll be worth watching." "Haven't you eaten yet?" I asked. "Come on, you can grab something in the street as we

總是三不沾，搶得猛一些，他就抽身出來，瞪着大眼看別人爭。文體幹事急得抓耳撓腮，大家又笑得前仰後合。每場下來，腳卵總是嚷野蠻，埋怨髒。

賽了兩天，決出總場各類運動代表隊，到地區參加地區決賽。大家看看王一生還沒有影子，就都相約要回去了。腳卵要留在地區文教書記家再待一兩天，就送我們走一段。快到街口，忽然有人一指：「那不是王一生？」大家順着方向一看，真是他。王一生在街另一面急急地走來，沒有看見我們。我們一齊大叫，他猛地站住，看見我們，就橫過街向我們跑來。到了跟前，大家紛紛問他怎麼不來參加比賽？王一生很着急的樣子，說：「這半年我總請事假出來下棋，等我知道報名趕回去，分場說我表現不好，不准我出來參加比賽，連名都沒報上。我剛找了由頭兒，跑上來看看賽得怎麼樣。怎麼樣？賽得怎麼樣？」大家一迭聲兒地說早賽完了，現在是參加與各縣代表隊的比賽，奪地區冠軍。

王一生愣了半晌，說：「也好，奪地區冠軍必是各縣高手，看看也不賴。」我說：「你還沒吃東西吧？走，街上隨便吃點什麼去。」腳

go." Legballs shook Wang Yisheng by the hand, full of sympathy for his plight. We all crowded into a small restaurant where we bought some food that we ate with many a sigh. "I want to watch the district chess tournament," said Wang Yisheng. "What about you lot? Are you going back?" The others said that they had to be getting back as they had been away for too long. "I'll stay here with you for another day or two," I said, "Legballs will be here too." Two or three of the others then also said that they'd hang around for another day or two.

Legballs led all of us who were staying in town off to the culture and education secretary's house, saying that he'd see if there was any chance that Wang Yisheng might be able to take part in the tournament. It did not take us long to get there. There was a small iron gate that was closed. When we went in we were asked who we were looking for, but once they saw Legballs, no more questions were asked and we were told to wait. A moment later we were called in, and we all trooped into the large house.

There was a row of well-tended plants on the window-sill. On the big wall was a hanging scroll of one of Chairman Mao's poems mounted on the palest of thin yellow silks. The only furniture in the room was a few cane chairs and a low table on which were several newspapers and some mimeographed reports. It was not long before the secretary came in, a fat man who shook each of us by the hand, called for somebody to take the mimeographed reports away, and invited us all to sit down. None of us had ever been into the home of a man who ruled several counties before, so we all peered around. The secretary was quiet for a moment before he asked, "Are you all fellow students of Ni Bin's?" We all turned back to look at the secretary, not knowing what to say. "They're all from our brigade," Legballs said, leaning forward. "This is Wang Yisheng," he continued, waving at him. "So you're Wang Yisheng, are you?" said the secretary, looking at him. "Good. Ni Bin has been talking about you a lot the last couple of days. Well, have you been selected for the district tournament?"

卵與王一生握過手，也惋惜不已。大家就又擁到一家小館兒，買了
一些飯菜，邊吃邊歎息。王一生説：「我是要看看地區的象棋大賽。
你們怎麼樣？要回去了嗎？」大家都説出來的時間太長了，要回去。
我説：「我再陪你一兩天吧。腳卵也在這裏。」於是又有兩三個人也
説留下來再耍一耍。

　　腳卵就領留下的人去文教書記家，説是看看王一生還有沒有參
加比賽的可能。走不多久，就到了。只見一扇小鐵門緊閉着，進去
就有人問找誰，見了腳卵，不再説什麼，只讓等一下。一會兒叫進
了，大家一起走進一幢大房子，

　　只見窗台上擺了一溜兒花草，伺候得很滋潤。大大的一面牆上
只一幅毛主席詩詞的掛軸兒，綾子黃黃的很淺。屋內只擺幾把藤
椅，茶几上放着幾張大報與油印的簡報。不一會兒，書記出來，胖
胖的，很快地與每個人握手，又叫人把簡報收走，就請大家坐下
來。大家沒見過管着幾個縣的人的家，頭都轉來轉去地看。書記呆
了一下，就問：「都是倪斌的同學嗎？」大家紛紛回過頭看書記，不
知該誰回答。腳卵欠一欠身，説：「都是我們隊上的。這一位就是王
一生。」説着用手掌向王一生一傾。書記看着王一生説：「噢，你就
是王一生？好。這兩天，倪斌常提到你。怎麼樣，選到地區來賽了
嗎？」

Wang Yisheng was just going to reply when Ni Bin cut in with. "Wang Yisheng was held up by a number of things he had to do, so he wasn't able to put his name down. He's done what he had to do now. Could he possibly get into the district tournament? What do you think?" The secretary's fat hands lightly patted the arms of his chair a couple of times, slowly and gently scratched the side of his nose. "Oh. So that's the way it is. It's tricky. It's tricky if you haven't qualified at the county level. I hear you're a genius, but people would complain if you were let into the tournament without having qualified." "I don't want to take part," said Wang Yisheng, his head bowed low, "I just want to watch." "That's OK," said the secretary. "You'd be most welcome. Ni Bin, go to the desk, the one on the left, and you'll find a duplicated schedule for the games. Bring it over and we'll see how the board games competitions have been organised."

Ni Bin stepped into the inner room and came straight out again with the papers. "The tournament lasts three days," he said when he had looked at them, then handed them to the secretary. The secretary put them on the table without looking at them, flicked them with his fingers and said, "Yes, there are several counties involved. Well? Any other problems?" We all stood up and said we had better be going. The secretary was very quick to shake hands with one of us who was nearest him and say, "Will you be coming over this evening, Ni Bin?" Ni Bin bowed and accepted, then left with the rest of us. Once out in the street we all breathed a sigh of relief and started talking and joking.

As we wandered aimlessly down the road we wondered whether we had enough money with us to stay here for three days. Wang Yisheng said he could find us somewhere to sleep, and there'd be no problem even though there were so many of us. Not staying in an inn would save us a lot of money. Ni Bin explained with some embarrassment that he would stay with the secretary. The rest of us went off with Wang Yisheng to find womewhere we could put up.

王一生正想答話，倪斌馬上就說：「王一生這次有些事耽誤了，沒有報上名。現在事情辦完了，看看還能不能參加地區比賽。您看呢？」書記用胖手在扶手上輕輕拍了兩下，又輕輕用中指很慢地擦着鼻溝兒，說：「啊，是這樣。不好辦。你沒有取得縣一級的資格，不好辦。聽說你很有天才，可是沒有取得資格去參加比賽，下面要說話的，啊？」王一生低了頭，說：「我也不是要參加比賽，只是來看看。」書記說：「那是可以的，那歡迎。倪斌，你去桌上，左邊的那個桌子，上面有一份打印的比賽日程。你拿來看看，象棋類是怎麼安排的。」

倪斌早一步跨進裏屋，馬上把材料拿出來，看了一下，說：「要賽三天呢！」就遞給書記。書記也不看，把它放在茶几上，撣一撣手，說：「是啊，幾個縣嘛。啊？還有什麼問題嗎？」大家都站起來，說走了。書記與離他近的人很快地握了手，說：「倪斌，你晚上來，嗯？」倪斌欠欠身說好的，就和大家一起出來。大家到了街上，舒了一口氣，說笑起來。

大家漫無目的地在街上走，講起還要在這裏呆三天，恐怕身上的錢支持不住。王一生說他可以找到睡覺的地方，人多一點恐怕還是有辦法，這樣就能不去住店，省下不少錢。倪斌不好意思地說他可以住在書記家。於是大家一起隨王一生去找住的地方。

Wang Yisheng had been to the district capital several times before, and he knew a painter who worked in the cultural centre. It was here that he led us all. When we reached the cultural centre and went inside, at once we could see people singing and playing instruments some distance away. We guessed that they must be the propaganda team rehearsing. Three or four women in blue knitted clothes, their breasts held about as high as they could be, wiggled their way up to us. As they came closer they did not make way for us at all, but went straight on without so much as a sideway glance. We moved to the side as quickly as we could, all blushing. "They're the district's star performers," whispered Ni Bin. "It's really something to have people as talented as them in an obscure place like this." We all looked back at the stars.

The painter lived in a tiny corner of the place with ducks and hens wandering in and out of the door. Bits and pieces were piled along the foot of the wall with weeds growing between them. The door was hidden by many clothes and cotton sheets hanging out to air. Wang Yisheng led us ducking through the clothes and called out the painter's name. Someone came clattering out at once, saw that it was Wang Yisheng and said, "It's you. Do all come in." The painter only had one little room with a narrow wooden bed in it. The room was full of books, magazines, paints, paper and brushes, and the walls were covered with pictures. We all trooped in, one after the other, and the painter moved his things about to make just enough room for us all to sit down, though we did not dare move. The painter made his way past all of us to go outside and come back a moment later with a thermos flask from which he poured us all some hot water. We passed each other mugs and bowls of every kind from which we all drank.

　　原來王一生已經來過幾次地區，認識了一個文化館畫畫兒的，於是便帶了我們投奔這位畫家。到了文化館，一進去，就聽見遠遠有唱的，有拉的，有吹的，便猜是宣傳隊在演練，只見三四個女的，穿着藍線衣褲，胸撅得不能再高，一扭一扭地走過來，近了，並不讓路，直脖直臉地過去。我們趕緊閃在一邊兒，都有點兒臉紅。倪斌低低地說：「這幾位是地區的名角。在小地方，有她們這樣的功夫，蠻不容易的。」大家就又回過頭去看名角。

　　畫家住在一個小角落裏，門口雞鴨轉來轉去，沿牆擺了一溜兒各類雜物，草就在雜物中間長出來。門又被許多曬着的衣褲布單遮住。王一生領我們從衣褲中彎腰過去，叫那畫家。馬上就乒乒乓乓出來一個人，見了王一生，說：「來了？都進來吧。」畫家只是一間小屋，裏面一張小木牀，到處是書、雜誌、顏色和紙筆。牆上釘滿了畫的畫兒。大家順序進去，畫家就把東西挪來挪去騰地方，大家擠着進去，不敢再動。畫家又邁過大家出去，一會兒提來一個暖瓶，給大家倒水。大家傳着各式的缸子、碗，都有了，捧着喝。

The painter sat down too and asked Wang Yisheng, "Are you taking part in the games?" Wang Yisheng gave a sigh and told him the whole story. "It's just as well," said the painter. "Are you going to stay for a few days?" "That's why I've come to see you," said Wang Yisheng. "These are all friends of mine. Could you find us somewhere where we could all squash in and sleep?" The painter thought for a while repying, "When you come you can squeeze in here with me and we get by. But this many ... mmm. Let me see." Then his eyes lit up and he said, "There's an auditorium in this cultural centre with a very big stage. There'll be a show tonight for the people taking part in the games, and you can sleep on the stage afterwards. How about it? I can even take you in to watch the show today. The electrician's a friend of mine. I'll have a word with him and there'll be no problem about going in and sleeping there. The only thing is that it's a bit dirty." We all said at once that it would be perfect. Legablls, evidently relieved, stood up carefully and said, "Fine, gentlemen. I'll be off." We all wanted to stand up to say goodbye to him but none of us was able to. Legballs held us down, repeatedly said that there was no need to get up, and stepped outside with a single stride. "He is really tall," the painter said. "Is he a basketball player?" We all burst out laughing and told him the funny story about Legballs. When the painter had heard it he said, "Yes, you're all filthy. Go and get washed. I'm coming with you." We all filed out in order, but still kept knocking noisily against things.

A river flowed past the district capital at some distance from it. We had to walk a long way before we reached it. It was not very wide, but the water flowed very fast, making little whirlpools near the bank. As there was nobody else anywhere around we all stripped right off and gave ourselves a really good wash, using up the cake of soap that the painter had brought with him. Then we soaked our clothes in the river, pounded them clean on boulders, wrung them out and spread them out on the rocks to dry. Apart from some who swam the rest of us

　　畫家也坐下來，問王一生：「參加運動會了嗎？」王一生歎着將
事情講了一遍。畫家說：「只好這樣了。要待幾天呢？」王一生就
說：「正是為這事來找你。這些都是我的朋友。你看能不能找個地
方，大家擠一擠睡？」畫家沉吟半晌，說：「你每次來，在我這裏擠
還湊合。這麼多人，嗯──讓我看看。」他忽然眼裏放出光來，說：
「文化館有個禮堂，舞台倒是很大。今天晚上為運動會的人演出，演
出之後，你們就在舞台上睡，怎麼樣？今天我還可以帶你們進去看
演出。電工與我很熟的，跟他說一聲，進去睡沒問題。只不過髒一
些。」大家都紛紛說再好不過了。腳卵放下心的樣子，小心地站起
來，說：「那好，諸位，我先走一步。」大家要站起來送，卻誰也站
不起來。腳卵按住大家，連說不必了，一腳就邁出屋外。畫家說：
「好大的個子！是打球的吧？」大家笑起來，講了腳卵的笑話。畫家
聽了，說：「是啊，你們也都夠髒的。走，去洗洗澡，我也去。」大
家就一個一個順序出去，還是碰得叮噹亂響。

　　原來這地區所在地，有一條江遠遠流過。大家走了許久，方才
到了。江面不甚寬闊，水卻很急，近岸的地方，有一些小窪兒。四
處無人，大家脫了衣褲，都很認真地洗，將畫家帶來的一塊肥皂用
完。又把衣褲泡了，在石頭上抽打，擰乾後鋪在石頭上曬，除了游
水的，其餘便紛紛趴在岸上曬。畫家早洗完，坐在一邊兒，掏出個
本子在畫。我發覺了，過去站在他身後看。原來他在畫我們幾個人

sunbathed on the bank. The painter, who had finished washing long before us, had brought out a sketchbook and was drawing. When I noticed this I went over and stood behind him to look. He was doing a nude sketch of us. The picture made me realise how remarkably strong we men who worked so hard in the mountains were and could not help sighing with admiration. Everyone else crowded round to look as well, their white bottoms flashing around. "People working have something very distinctive about the lines of their muscles. They're very clear visible. Even though the development of the different parts isn't always very even, real bodies are often like that, infinitely varied. When I did life studies at art college they were mostly of women, but they tended to be too standard. The male models were usually stationary too: you got no feel of moving muscle, and the more you painted them the deader it all was. Today's a rare opportunity." Some of them said that their private parts were not nice to look at, whereupon the painter used his pencil to turn their privates in the picture into a big lump, which made everyone laugh. By now our clothes were dry and we all climbed back into them.

It was almost dusk, and the sun was setting between two mountains, making the river ripple with gold and turning the rocks on the bank as red as hot iron. Birds were darting across the water with cries that could be heard from far away. On the opposite bank someone was singing a long-drawn-out folksong: we could not see him, but we could hear his voice gradually fading away. We all gazed in rapt concentration. After a long time Wang Yisheng sighed but said nothing.

We all went back, and along the way we dragged the painter out to have something to eat with us. He turned out to be quite a drinker. It was now dark, and he took us in through the stage door of the auditorium, where he gave someone a nod, had a word wit him, and gestured to us to go in very quietly, hide in the wings and watch from

的裸體速寫。經他這一畫，我倒發現我們這些每日在山上苦的人，卻矯健異常，不禁讚歎起來。大家又圍過來看，屁股白白的晃來晃去。畫家說：「幹活兒的人，肌肉線條極有特點，又很分明。雖然各部分發展可能不太平衡，可真的人體，常常是這樣，變化萬端。我以前在學院畫人體，女人體居多，太往標準處靠，男人體也常靜在那裏，感覺不出肌肉滾動，越畫越死。今天真是個難得的機會。」有人說羞處不好看，畫家就在紙上用筆把說的人的羞處塗成一個疙瘩，大家就都笑起來。衣褲乾了，紛紛穿上。

這時已近傍晚，太陽垂在兩山之間，江面上便金子一般滾動，岸邊石頭也如熱鐵般紅起來。有鳥兒在水面上掠來掠去，叫聲傳得很遠。對岸有人在拖長聲音吼山歌，卻不見影子，只覺聲音慢慢小了。大家都凝了神看。許久，王一生長歎一聲，卻不說什麼。

大家又都往回走，在街上拉了畫家一起吃些東西，畫家倒好酒量。天黑了，畫家領我們到禮堂後台入口，與一個人點頭說了，招呼大家悄悄進去，縮在邊幕上看。時間到了，幕並不開，說是書記

there. The curtains did not open when they were supposed to because, it was said, the secretary had not yet arrived. The performers, all dressed and made up, were walking to and fro backstage, stretching and joking with each other. Suddenly there was a noise in the house. I lifted a corner of the curtain to see the fat secretary make a leisurely entrance and sit in the front row. All around him were empty seats, behind which the auditorium was a densely crowded mass of people. The show now began. It was a very impassioned performance that raised clouds of dust everywhere.

Onstage the performers had tears in their eyes, but once they were in the wings they all started giggling and going on about all the things that had gone wrong. But Wang Yisheng was completely carried away by the show. Sometimes his face was overcast and at other times he looked happy, and his mouth was gaping open all the way through. The calmness with which he played chess had vanished completely. When the show ended he started applauding all by himself from the wings. I stopped him at once and looked down from the stage. The front two rows were once again empty. The secretary had left some time earlier.

We all went outside and groped our way through the dark to the painter's room. Legballs was there before us, and as soon as he saw us coming he came out with the painter to stand outside. "Wang Yisheng," the painter said, "you can take part in the tournament." "How's that?" Wang Yisheng asked. Legballs explained that when he had been at the secretary's home earlier that evening the secretary had mentioned in the course of a social conversation that a dozen or so years ago he had often visited Legballs' home and seen a lot of paintings and calligraphy there. He wondered if they had been lost since the movement had started. Legballs had replied that they still had some left, after which the secretary had said nothing else. A little later the secretary had added that there should no be any problem about Legballs' transfer: he could

還未來。演員們都化了妝，在後台走來走去，抻一抻手腳，互相取笑着。忽然外面響動起來，我撥了幕布一看，只見書記緩緩進來，在前排坐下，周圍空着，後面黑壓壓一禮堂人。於是開演，演出甚為激烈，塵土四起。

演員們在台上淚光閃閃，退下來一過邊幕，就喜笑顏開，連說怎麼怎麼錯了。王一生倒很入戲，臉上時陰時晴，嘴一直張着，全沒有在棋盤前的鎮靜。戲一結束，王一生一個人在邊幕拍起手來，我連忙止住他，向台下望去，書記不知什麼時候已經走了，前兩排仍然空着。

大家出來，摸黑拐到畫家家裏，腳卵已在屋裏，見我們來了，就與畫家出來和大家在外面站着，畫家說：「王一生，你可以參加比賽。」王一生問：「怎麼回事兒？」腳卵說，晚上他在書記家裏，書記跟他說起家常，說十幾年前常去他家，見過不少字畫兒，不知運動起來，損失了沒有？腳卵說還有一些，書記就不說話了。過了一會兒書記又說，腳卵的調動大約不成問題，到地區文教部門找個位

find a place for him in a culture or education office in the district capital. He would have a word with his subordinates and it could all be done quickly. He hoped that Legballs would write home about it. The secretary then turned the conversation back to calligraphy, paintings and antiques. People didn't know the value of such things these days, he said, but he often thought about them. Legballs had said that he would write home to see if they could give one or two scrolls to the secretary, who deserved thanks for being so very helpful. He had also said he had a superb Ming chess set in ebony back in his brigade. If the secretary liked the sound of it he could bring it with him next time. This had got the secretary very excited: he had repeatedly urged Legballs to bring it along to let him have a look. Then the secretary had mentioned Legballs' friend Wang Yisheng. He could have a word with his subordinates. It was only a district tournament: there was no need to be too strict. After all, when it came to real talent you did not have to avoid recommending your friends. He had then made a phone call and been told that there would be no problem. The secretary need not worry. Wang Yisheng could take part in the tournament the next day.

We were all very pleased to hear this and said that Legballs was a real operator. Wang Yisheng said nothing. When Legballs had gone the painter took us all off to find the electrician, who opened the stage door of the auditorium and let us go quietly in. He offered to let us take the curtains down to use as blankets as the weather had now turned cool. We all jumped at the chance and climbed up to take the curtains down and spread them out in the stage. One of our group walked to the front of the stage, bowed to the empty seats and declared in the strident tones of an announcer, "The next item, now beginning, will be—sleep." We all had a quiet laugh then crawled under the curtain and lay down.

置,跟下面打個招呼,辦起來也快,讓腳卵寫信回家講一講。於是又談起字畫古董,說大家現在都不知道這些東西的價值,書記自己倒是常在心裏想着。腳卵就說,他寫信給家裏,看能不能送書記一兩幅,既然書記幫了這麼大忙,感謝是應該的。又說,自己在隊裏有一副明朝的烏木棋,極是考究,書記若是還看得上,下次帶下來。書記很高興,連說帶上來看看。又說你的朋友王一生,他倒可以和下面的人說一說,一個地區的比賽,不必那麼嚴格,舉賢不避私嘛。就掛了電話,電話裏回答說,沒有問題,請書記放心,叫王一生明天就參加比賽。

大家聽了,都很高興,稱讚腳卵路道粗。王一生卻沒說話。腳卵走後,畫家帶了大家找到電工,開了禮堂後門,悄悄進去。電工說天涼了,問要不要把幕布放下來墊蓋着?大家都說好,就七手八腳爬上去摘下幕布鋪在台上。一個人走到台邊,對着空空的座位一敬禮,尖着嗓子學報幕員,說:「下一個節目——睡覺。現在開始。」大家悄悄地笑,紛紛鑽進幕布躺下了。

After I had been lying there for a long time I noticed that Wang Yisheng was still awake. "Go to sleep," I said, "you've got the tournament tomorrow." "I'm not going in for it," he replied in the darkness. "There's no point. It's ever so kind of Ni Bin, but I don't want to go in for it." "What are you worrying about?" I said. "You get into the tournament and he gets transferred here. A chess set's nothing." "But it's his father's chess set," said Wang Yisheng. "It's not the quality of it that counts but what it means. I've always guarded the chess set without any writing on it that my mother left me like my life; and I can't forget what she told me now that my life's easier. How can Ni Bin give the set away?" "Legballs' people have got loads of money," I replied. "What's a chess set to them? If it means their son can have an easier time they'll be glad to part with it." "Say what you will, I'm not going for it," answered Wang Yisheng. "It'd look as though I was cashing in on someone else's deal. Whether I win or lose should only depend on me. If I payed on those terms there'd be someone jabbing at my conscience." One of the others, who was still awake and had probably heard all that we had said, mumbled, "You really are a maniac."

　　躺下許多，我發覺王一生還沒有睡着，就說：「睡吧，明天要
參加比賽呢！」王一生在黑暗裏説：「我不賽了，沒意思。倪斌是好
心，可我不想賽了。」我説：「咳，管它！你能賽棋，腳卵能調上
來，一副棋算什麼？」王一生説：「那是他父親的棋呀！東西好壞不
説，是個信物。我媽留給我的那副無字棋，我一直性命一樣存着，
現在生活好了，媽的話，我也忘不了。倪斌怎麼就可以送人呢？」
我説：「腳卵家裏有錢，一副棋算什麼呢？他家裏知道兒子活得好
一些了，棋是捨得的。」王一生説：「我反正是不賽了，被人作了交
易，倒像是我佔了便宜。我下得贏下不贏是我自己的事，這樣賽，
被人戳脊樑骨。」不知是誰也沒睡着，大約都聽見了，咕嚕一聲：
「呆子。」

4

First thing the next morning we all got up, covered in dirt, and found some water to wash in. After that we tried to get the painter to come out for a meal with us. He insisted on refusing, and as we were talking Legballs turned up looking in very high spirits. "I'm not going in for the tournament," Wang Yisheng told him. Everyone was dumbfounded. "That's just great," said Legballs. "Why won't you? People are coming from the provincial capital to watch." "I won't, and that's that," said Wang Yisheng. When I explained why Legballs sighed and said, "The secretary's a cultured man who's very crazy about that sort of thing. Although the set's a family heirloom I really can't take life on the farm. All I want is to be able to live somewhere clean where I won't get filthy dirty every day. I can't eat a chess set. If it'll get me over a few obstacles it's worth it. My parents aren't very well off: they won't blame me."

The painter folded his arms, rubbed his cheek with one hand, looked up at the sky and said, "Ideals have all gone: all that's left is ambition. I don't blame you, Ni Bin. Your demands are nothing very much. In the last couple of years I've often done stupid things. My life is too much tied up with trivialities. Luckily I can still paint. What is there to ease melancholy, save ..." He sighed. Wang Yisheng gazed at him in astonishment, then slowly turned towards Legballs and said,

四

　　第二天一早兒，大家滿身是土地起來，找水擦了擦，又約畫家到街上去吃。畫家執意不肯，正說着，腳卵來了，很高興的樣子。王一生對他說：「我不參加這個比賽。」大家呆了，腳卵問：「蠻好的，怎麼不賽了呢？省裏還下來人視察呢！」王一生說：「不賽就不賽了。」我說了說，腳卵歎道：「書記是個文化人，蠻喜歡這些的。棋雖然是家裏傳下的，可我實在受不了農場這個罪，我只想有個乾淨的地方住一住，不要每天髒兮兮的。棋不能當飯吃的，用它通一些關節，還是值的。家裏也不很景氣，不會怪我。」

　　畫家把雙臂抱在胸前，抬起一隻手摸了摸臉，看着天說：「倪斌，不能怪你。你沒有什麼了不得的要求。我這兩年，也常常犯糊塗，生活太具體了。幸虧我還會畫畫兒。何以解憂？唯有——唉。」王一生很驚奇地看着畫家，慢慢轉了臉對腳卵說：「倪斌，謝謝你。

"Thank you, Legballs. As soon as it's obvious who the best players in the tournament are I'll challenge them. But I won't take part in the tournament." Legballs cheered up at once, clenched his enormous hand for a moment and said, "I've got it. I'll go and have a word with the secretary and get him to organise a friendly match. If you can beat the champion you'll unquestionably be the real champ. And even if you lose it won't be too much of a loss of face." Wang Yisheng paused then said, "Don't say anything to the secretary, whatever you do. I'll get them to play myself. If they'll agree I'll take the top three on together."

None of us knew what to say after that, so we went off to watch the games. It was fun. Wang Yisheng made his way to the hall where the board games were being played and watched the big scoreboards on which all the games were set out for spectators. On the third day the winner and the two runners-up emerged. After that the prizes were awarded, there was another performance, and the place was so noisy and chaotic that you could not hear who had won what.

Legballs told us to wait where the games were being held and came back a little later with two men in blue cadre uniforms. He introduced them as the second and third prize-winners in the chess tournament. "This is Wang Yisheng," he continued. "He's a terrific player and he'd like to have a game with you two distinguished players. It'll be a chance for you all to learn from each other." The two of them looked at Wang Yisheng and asked, "Why didn't you go in for the tournament? We've been hanging around here for ages and we've got to go back." "I won't keep you waiting," said Wang Yisheng. "I'll play you both at the same time." The two of them looked at each other, then the penny droped. "Playing blind?" they asked. Wang Yisheng nodded. The two of them changed their attitude now. "We've never played blind," they said with apologetic smiles. "Doesn't matter," said Wang Yisheng. "You two can have boards to look at while you play. Come on, let's find somewhere."

這次比賽決出高手，我登門去與他們下。我不參加這次比賽了。」腳卵忽然很興奮，攘起大手一頓，說：「這樣，這樣！我呢，去跟書記說一下，組織一個友誼賽。你要是贏了這次的冠軍，無疑是真正的冠軍。輸了呢，也不太失身份。」王一生呆了呆：「千萬不要跟什麼書記說，我自己找他們下。要下，就與前三名都下。」

大家也不好再說什麼，就去看各種比賽，倒也熱鬧。王一生只鑽在棋類場地外面，看各局的明棋。第三天，決出前三名。之後是發獎，又是演出，會場亂哄哄的，也聽不清誰得的是什麼獎。

腳卵讓我們在會場等着，過了不久，就領來兩個人，都是制服打扮。腳卵作了介紹，原來是象棋比賽的第二三名。腳卵說：「這位是王一生，棋蠻厲害的，想與你們兩位高手下一下，大家也是一個互相學習的機會。」兩個人看了看王一生，問：「那怎麼不參加比賽呢？我們在這裏呆了許多天，要回去了。」王一生說：「我不耽誤你們，與他們兩人同時下。」兩人互相看了看，忽然悟到，說：「盲棋？」王一生點一點頭。兩人立刻變了態度，笑着說：「我們沒下過盲棋。」王一生說：「不要緊，你們看着明棋下。來，咱們找個地方兒。」

Somehow or other the news got out, and it created an immediate stir. The people from all the different counties who had come to the games told each other that some whipper-snapper from a state farm who hadn't gone in for the tournament wouldn't accept the result and wanted to play the runner-up and the man in third place at the same time. A good hundred people crowded round us, pushing and shoving to get a look. We all felt responsible for Wang Yisheng and stood around him. Wang Yisheng bowed his head and said, "Let's go, let's go. We're attracting too much attention here." Someone pushed through and asked, "Which of you wants to play chess? You? Our uncle won this championship. He's heard that you aren't happy about the result and has sent me to invite you over." "That won't be necessary," said Wang Yisheng. "If you uncle would like to play I'll take all three of you on at once."

This caused a sensation among the onlookers, who all headed to the chess hall with us. There were over a hundred people all marching along the street with us in a crowd, which set the passers-by asking what was up and wondering if the school leavers were going to have a brawl. When they found out what was happening they tagged along too. By the time we had gone half way down the street there were upward of a thousand people milling round. Assistants and customers alike came out of the shops to see what was going on. The long-distance bus had to go this way but could not get through: the passengers craned their heads out to stare. The street was a sea of heads. Clouds of dust were rising, and amid the general hubbub was the scrunch of waste paper being trodden underfoot. A halfwit stood in the middle of the street singing a wordless howl of a song until someone had the charity to pull him out of the way. The idiot went on with his song beside the wall. Four or five dogs rushed around, barking as if they were leading a wolf hunt.

　　話不知怎麼就傳了出去，立刻嚷動了，會場上各縣的人都說有一個農場的小子沒有賽着，不服氣，要同時與亞、季軍比試。百十個人把我們圍了起來，擠來擠去地看，大家覺得有了責任，便站在王一生身邊兒。王一生倒低了頭，對兩個人說：「走吧，走吧，太扎眼。」有一個人擠了進來，說：「哪個要下棋？就是你嗎？我們大爺這次是冠軍，聽說你不服氣，叫我來請你。」王一生慢慢地說：「不必。你大爺要是肯下，我和你們三人同下。」

　　眾人都轟動了，擁着往棋場走去。到了街上，百十人走成一片。行人見了，紛紛問怎麼回事，可是知青打架？待明白了，就都跟着走。走過半條街，竟有上千人跟着跑來跑去。商店裏的店員和顧客也都站出來張望。長途車路過這裏開不過，乘客們紛紛探出頭來，只見一街人頭攢動，塵土飛起多高，轟轟的，亂紙踏得嚓嚓響。一個傻子呆呆地在街中心，咿咿呀呀地唱，有人發了善心，把他拖開，傻子就依了牆根兒唱。四五條狗竄來竄去，覺得是它們在引路打狼，汪汪叫着。

By the time we reached the chess hall there were several thousand people around us. The cloud of dust they had raised would take a long time to settle. The slogans and signs at the hall had already been taken down. A man came out and blanched at the sight of so large a crowd. Legballs went over to negotiate with him. He took a quick look at all the people, nodded repeatedly, and took a long time to realise that they wanted to use the hall. He hurriedly opened the door, and kept saying. "Yes, yes," but when he saw that they all wanted to come in he became anxious. We stood guard at the entrance and only admitted Legballs, Wang Yisheng and the two prize winners.

Just then someone emerged from the crowd and said to us, "If the master is willing to play three people at once, one more won't matter. I can be one of them." There was another commotion in the crowd and someone else volunteered. I did not know what to do and had to go inside to tell Wang Yisheng. He chewed his lips then asked, "What do you two think about it?" The two of them stood up and agreed straight away. I went outside to count, and including the champion there were ten opponents altogether. "Ten's unlucky; it's a round number," said Legballs. "Nine would be better." So the number was kept down to nine. The champion had not arrived, but someone came to tell us that as it was blind chess that was being played the champion would stay at home and have messengers pass the moves on. Wang Yisheng thought for a moment then agreed. The nine of them were then shut inside the hall. As one chess board outside the hall was not enough to show the moves made, eight fullsized sheets of paper were fetched and marked out with the chessboard grid. Hundreds of square chessmen were cut out of card, painted with the names of the different pieces in red or in black, and given string tags on the back by which they were hung up at intersections on the grids. When the wind blew they fluttered gently, to roars from the crowds in the street.

　　到了棋場，竟有數千人圍住，土揚在半空，許久落不下來。棋場的標語標誌早已摘除，出來一個人，見這麼多人，臉都白了。腳卵上去與他交涉，他很快地看着眾人，連連點頭兒，半天才明白是借場子用，急忙打開門，連說「可以可以」，見眾人都要進去，就急了。我們幾個，馬上到門口守住，放進腳卵、王一生和兩個得了榮譽的人。

　　這時有一個走出來，對我們說：「高手既然和三個人下，多我一個不怕，我也算一個。」眾人又嚷動了，又有人報名。我不知怎麼辦好，只得進去告訴王一生。王一生咬一咬嘴說：「你們兩個怎麼樣？」那兩個人趕緊站起來，連說可以。我出去統計了，連冠軍在內，對手共是十人。腳卵說：「十不吉利的，九個人好了。」於是就九個人。冠軍總不見來，有人來報，既是下盲棋，冠軍只在家裏，命人傳棋。王一生想了想，說好吧。九個人就關在場裏。牆外一副明棋不夠用，於是有人拿來八張整開白紙，很快地畫了格兒。又有人用硬紙剪了百十個方棋子兒，用紅黑顏色寫了，背後粘上細繩，掛在棋格兒的釘子上，風一吹，輕輕地晃成一片，街上人們也嚷成一片。

More and more people were still arriving. Hard though the latecomers pushed they could not squeeze through the crowd, so they grabbed hold of others and asked what was going on, imagining that an execution announcement had been posted. Much further back there was another circle, this one made up of women holding children in their arms. Many other people had put their bicycle stands down and were standing on the rear carriers of their machines and craning their necks to look. With all the pushing and shoving a whole lot of people fell over amid many shouts. Older children were squeezing their way through and being pushed out again by adults' legs. The hubbub of the thousands of people made the street seem to rumble with thunder.

Wang Yisheng was sitting in the middle of the enclosure on a chair with a back, his hands on his legs and his eyes staring blankly. His face and hair were utterly filthy, making him look like a criminal brought in for interrogation. I could not help bursting out laughing, and I went across to brush some of the dirt off him. He pressed on my hand, so that I could feel him trembling. "It's getting out of hand," Wang Yisheng said very quietly. "You and your friends keep an eye on things. If there's any trouble we'll make a break for it together." "There won't be," I replied. "As long as you win there'll be no problem. You'll be able to hold your head high. Well? Are you sure you can cope with nine of them? Including the first three in the tournament?" Wang Yisheng was silent for a while before he replied, "What I'm scared of are the players from the wilds, not the men from the court. I've seen how the people in the tournament play, but there's no way of telling that I won't find my match among the other six. Take my satchel, and whatever happens don't lose it. I've got ... " he gave me a look "my mother's chessmen in it". His skinny face was both dry and dirty, and even the sides of his nose were black. His hair was standing upright, and as his throat moved his eyes looked alarmingly dark. I realised that he was putting everything he had into these games and felt very anxious. "Be careful," was all I said as I left him, alone in the middle of the enclosure, looking at nobody. He was as still as a lump of iron.

人是愈來愈多。後來的人拚命往前擠，擠不進去，就抓住人打聽，以為是殺人的告示。婦女們也抱着孩子們，遠遠圍成一片。又有許多人支了自行車，站在後架上伸脖子看，人群一擠，連着倒，喊成一團。半大的孩子們鑽來鑽去，被大人們用腿拱出去。數千人鬧鬧嚷嚷，街上像半空響着悶雷。

王一生坐在場當中一個靠背椅上，把手放在兩條腿上，眼睛虛望着，一頭一臉都是土，像是被傳訊的歹人。我不禁笑起來，過去給他拍一拍土。他按住我的手，我覺出他有些抖。王一生低低地說：「事情鬧大了。你們幾個朋友看好，一有動靜，一起跑。」我說：「不會。只要你贏了，什麼都好辦。爭口氣。怎麼樣？有把握嗎？九個人哪！頭三名都在這裏！」王一生沉吟了一下，說：「怕江湖的不怕朝廷的，參加過比賽的人的棋路我都看了，就不知道其他六人會不會冒出冤家。書包你拿着，不管怎麼樣，書包不能丟。書包裏有……」王一生看了看我：「我媽的無字棋。」他的瘦臉上又乾又髒，鼻溝兒也黑了，頭髮立着，喉嚨一動一動的，兩眼黑得嚇人。我知道他拚了，心裏有些酸，只說：「保重！」就離了他。他一個人空空地在場中央，誰也不看，靜靜的像一塊鐵。

The chess began. A hush fell upon the crowd of thousands. The only words came from the volunteers who were calling the moves out, sometimes fast and sometimes slow, for the volunteers outside to move the pieces on the eight big boards. The boards were rustling in the breeze, which set the pieces fluttering. The setting sun shone on everything with a dazzling glare. The front few dozen rows had all sat down and were looking up, while the people behind them were packed close together, all looking filthy dirty and with their hair, long or short, blowing in the wind. Nobody else moved. It was as if they were all fighting for their lives in the chess games.

Something very ancient suddenly welled up in my heart, which rose in my throat. Of all the books I had read some came close to me, some moved away. Everything was muddled up. Xiang Yu and Liu Bang, those legendary generals of over two thousand years ago I so much admired, were glaring at each other in stupefied fury. But the dark-faced soldiers whose corpses littered the plain were rising from the ground and slowly moving, not making a sound. A woodcutter was holding his axe and singing wildly. Then I seemed to see the Chess Maniac's mother folding printed sheets one at a time with her feeble hands.

I found myself feeling inside Wang Yisheng's satchel. My fingers gripped a little cotton bundle that I took out to examine. It was a little bag made of worn blue twill that had been embroidered with a bat. The corners had been sewn into scallops with very fine stitching. I brought out one of the chessmen. It really was very small and in the sunlight half translucent, like the gentle look of an eye. I held it tight in my hand.

The sun finally set, bringing immediate coolness. People were still watching, but they had now started discussing the game. Every time one of Wang Yisheng's moves was called out from inside the hall there

　　棋開始了。上千人不再出聲兒。只有自願服務的人一會兒緊一會兒慢地用話傳出棋步，外邊兒自願服務的人就變動着棋子兒。風吹得八張大紙嘩嘩地響。棋子兒蕩來蕩去。太陽斜斜地照在一切上，燒得耀眼。前幾十排的人都坐下了，仰起頭看，後面的人也擠得緊緊的，一個個土眉土眼，頭髮長長短短吹得飄，再沒有動一下，似乎都把命放在棋裏搏。

　　我心裏忽然有一種很古的東西湧上來，喉嚨緊緊地往上走。讀過的書，有的近了，有的遠了，模糊了，平時十分佩服的項羽、劉邦都目瞪口呆，倒是屍橫遍野的那些黑臉士兵，從地下爬起來，啞了喉嚨，慢慢移動。一個樵夫，提了斧在野唱。忽然又彷彿見了呆子的母親，用一雙弱手一張一張地摺書頁。

　　我不由伸手到王一生的書包裏去掏摸，捏到一個小布包兒，拽出來一看，是個舊藍斜紋布的小口袋，上面用線繡了一隻蝙蝠，布的四邊兒都用線做了圈口，針腳很是細密。取出一個棋子，確實很小，在太陽底下竟是半透明的，像是一隻眼睛，正柔和地瞧着。我把它攥在手裏。

　　太陽終於落下去，立刻爽快了。人們仍在看着，但議論起來。裏邊兒傳出一句王一生的棋步，外邊兒的人就嚷動一下。專有幾個

was a murmur in the crowd outside. There were several messengers carrying the moves to and from the champion's home by bicycle. We were no longer on our best behaviour, and had started joking and talking.

 I went back inside to see Legballs looking very excited, which made me feel a lot less tense. "Well then?" I said. "I can't understand chess." "it's terrific," said Legballs, stroking his hair, "terrific. I've never seen anything like it. Just think: one man against nine; nine games at once. A huge campaign on a 360-degree front. I'm going to write to my father and tell him all the moves in all the games." Just then two men stood up from their boards, bowed to Wang Yisheng, and said, "You're too good for us." They went outside, kneading their hands. Wang Yisheng gave a nod and glanced at their boards.

Wang Yisheng had not changed his position. He still had his hands on his knees and was gazing straight in front of him. He might have been looking into the furthest distance, or staring at something extremely close to him. A large jacket was draped over his skinny shoulders. He was still covered with patches of dirt that had not been brushed off. It was a long time before his Adam's apple moved. For the first time I accepted that chess too was an athletic activity—a marathon, a double marathon. I had done some long distance running at school. After five hundred metres I had felt exhausted, but after passing a certain limit my brain had no longer been involved in running. I had become like a pilotless aircraft or a glider that had reached a great height and was just gliding down. But chess was an athletic activity in which you had to use your intelligence from beginning to end to fight your opponent and wrestle him into submission. You could never be careless for a moment.

I was struck with anxiety about Wang Yisheng's health. Because we were so hard up we had not eaten very well during the previous

人騎車為在家的冠軍傳送着棋步，大家就不太客氣，笑話起來。

我又進去，看見腳卵很高興的樣子，心裏就鬆開一些，問：「怎麼樣？我不懂棋。」腳卵抹一抹頭髮，說：「蠻好，蠻好。這種陣勢，我從來也沒見過，你想想看，九個人與他一個人下，九局連環！車輪大戰！我要寫信給我的父親，把這次的棋譜都寄給他。」這時有兩個人從各自的棋盤前站起來，朝着王一生一鞠躬，說：「甘拜下風。」就捏着手出去了。王一生點點頭兒，看了他們的位置一眼。

王一生的姿勢沒有變，仍舊是雙手扶膝，眼平視着，像是望着極遠極遠的遠處，又像是盯着極近極近的近處，瘦瘦的肩挑着寬大的衣服，土沒拍乾淨，東一塊兒，西一塊兒。喉節許久才動一下。我第一次承認象棋也是運動，而且是馬拉松，是多一倍的馬拉松！我在學校時，參加過長跑，開始後的五百米，確實極累，但過了一個限度，就像不是在用腦子跑，而像一架無人駕駛飛機，又像是一架到了高度的滑翔機，只管滑翔下去。可這象棋，終於是處在一種機敏的運動之中，兜捕對手，逼向死角，不能疏忽。

我忽然擔心起王一生的身體來。這幾天，大家因為錢緊，不敢怎麼吃，晚上睡得又晚，誰也沒想到會有這麼一個場面。看着王一

few days and had gone to bed very late, never imagining that anything like this was in store. As I looked at Wang Yisheng sitting so steady there I felt a surge of sympathy for him: "Hold on!" When we were carrying logs in the mountains, two of us to a log, and even if the paths were lousy and the valleys turned out to be dead ends we gritted our teeth and never gave up. If either of you collapsed because you could not take it you would of course be injured yourself, and your partner would be hit so hard by the log that he would vomit blood afterwards. But this time Wang Yisheng had to cross the creeks and gullies by himself: we could not help him at all. I fetched some cold water that I quietly took to him and held up in front of his face. He shook, looked at me with eyes like swords, and took some time to recognise me and give me a joyless smile. I pointed at the bowl of water, which he took and was about to drink from when a messenger came to report a move to him. He raised the bowl till it was level with his eyes, making not a ripple and gazed at the rim of the bowl as he announced his own move. Then he moved the bowl slowly to his lips. Just then the next messenger reported another move. His mouth stayed fixed at the rim of the bowl as he said what his move was. Only then did he swallow a mouthful of water with a terrifyingly loud noise. There were tears in his eyes. He passed the bowl back, gazing at me with a look in which there was something bittersweet that could never have been put into words. A trickle of water ran slowly down from the corner of his mouth that washed a channel through the dirt on his chin and his neck. I handed the bowl back to him. He raised his hand to stop me and returned to his world.

When I came out it was dark. Some of the mountain folk were holding torches of burning pine and other people had electric torches, which all made a mass of bright yellow light. Probably the district offices had just finished work as there were more people there than ever. Dogs were sitting in front of the people watching with mournful

生穩穩地坐在那裏，我又替他賭一口氣：死頂吧！我們在山上扛木料，兩個人一根，不管路不是路，溝不是溝，也得咬牙，死活不能放手。誰若是頂不住軟了，自己傷了不說，另一個也得被木頭震得吐血。可這回是王一生一個人過溝過坎兒，我們幫不上忙。我找了點兒涼水來，悄悄走近他，在他眼前一擋，他抖了一下，眼睛刀子似的看了我一下，一會兒才認出是我，就乾乾地笑了一下。我指指水碗，他接過去，正要喝，一個局號報了棋步。他把碗高高地平端着，水紋絲兒不動。他看着碗邊兒，回報了棋步，就把碗緩緩湊到嘴邊兒。這時下一個局號又報了棋步，他把嘴定在碗邊兒，半晌，回報了棋步，才咽一口水下去，「咕」的一聲兒，聲音大得可怕，眼裏有了淚花。他把碗遞過來，眼睛望望我，有一種說不出的東西在裏面遊動，嘴角兒緩緩流下一滴水，把下巴和脖子上的土沖開一道溝兒。我又把碗遞過去，他豎起手掌止住我，回到他的世界裏去了。

我出來，天已黑了。有山民打着松枝火把，有人用手電照着，黃乎乎的，一團明亮。大約是地區的各種單位下班了，人更多了，狗也在人前蹲着，看人掛動棋子，眼神淒淒的，像是在擔憂。幾個

expressions as the hanging chessmen were moved: it was as if they understood and were worried. Several of the school-leavers in our brigade were surrounded by people asking them questions. Before long the information was being passed on: "Wang Yisheng", "the Chess Maniac", "an educated youngster", "he plays Taoist chess" and so on. I found this laughable and wanted to go into the crowd and explain, but then I stopped myself: let them pass it on, I thought. At this point I started feeling happy. There were only three games still being played out on the wall.

Suddenly a roar went up from the crowd. I looked round and saw that there was only one game now, the game with the champion. There were few pieces left on the board. Wang Yisheng's black pieces were all in his opponnent's half of the board apart from his commander, which had an officer to keep him company. They were like an emperor and his courtier talking while waiting for the army at the front to send back the report of victory. You could almost make out servants preparing a banquet and lighting foot-long red candles while the musical instruments were being tuned, ready to burst out into triumphant music as soon as the messenger fell to his knees to announce the victory. My stomach gave a long rumble and my legs felt weak. I chose somewhere and sat down, gazing up at the final hunt, terrified that something might go wrong.

The red pieces had not moved for a long time, and the crowd was looking out for the arrival of the cyclist with a general buzz of impatience. Suddenly the people in the crowd started moving about and opening a way through. An old man with a bald head slowly walked out of the crowd, helped by those around him. As he examined the boards on which the endings of the other eight games were displayed his lips moved. Everyone spread the news that this was the man who had just won the district championship, a member of a distinguished local family who had emerged from his seclusion just

同來的隊上知青，各被人圍了打聽。不一會兒，「王一生」、「棋呆子」、「是個知青」、「棋是道家的棋」，就在人們嘴上傳。我有些發噱，本想到人群裏説説，但又止住了，隨人們傳吧，我開始高興起來。這時牆上只有三局在下了。

忽然人群發一聲喊。我回頭一看，原來只剩了一盤，恰是與冠軍的那一盤，盤上只有不多幾個子兒。王一生的黑子兒遠遠近近地峙在對方棋營格裏，後方老帥穩穩地呆着，尚有一「士」伴着，好像帝王與近侍在聊天兒，等着前方將幹得勝回朝；又似乎隱隱看見有人在伺候酒宴，點起尺把長的紅蠟燭，有人在悄悄地調整管弦，單等有人跪奏捷報，鼓樂齊鳴。我的肚子拖長了音兒在響，腳下覺得軟了，就揀個地方坐下，仰頭看最後的圍獵，生怕有什麼差池。

紅子兒半天不動，大家不耐煩了，紛紛看騎車的人來沒來，嗡嗡地響成一片。忽然人群亂起來，紛紛閃開。只見一老者，精光頭皮，由旁人攙着，慢慢走出來，嘴嚼動着，上上下下看着八張定局殘子。眾人紛紛傳着，這就是本屆地區冠軍，是這個山區的一個世

to play chess for fun, never expecting to take first place. His comment on the tournament had been to sigh for the decline of chess. When he had examined all the games he gave his clothes a gentle tug, stamped, raised his head and was helped into the chess hall. The crowd pushed in after him. I pushed my way anxiously towards the entrance as I followed behind. The old man went inside, stopped and looked in front of him.

Wang Yisheng was sitting alone in the big room, staring towards us, his hands on his knees, a slender pillar of iron who seemed to hear and see nothing. An electric light high above him shone dimly on his face. His eyes were sunken, and very dark. It was as if they were looking up at an infinite number of worlds, at the vastness of the universe. All his life force seemed to be concentrated in his mop of tousled hair. For a long time it did not disperse, then it gradually spread out, burning our faces.

They were all astounded and said nothing. After everything that had been said outside for so long they were now faced with a black, skinny little soul sitting there in perfect stillness. They all gasped.

After a while the old man gave a very full and deep cough that resonated round the room. Wang Yisheng suddenly shortened the focus of his gaze, saw the crowd and tried to get up, but be could not move. The old man shook off the people who were supporting him and took a few steps forward, stopped, gently stroked his chest with both hands, and said in a loud, clear voice, "Young man, I am old and infirm, which was why I could not come here to play with you. I had no option but to ask messengers to pass on the moves. I can see that despite your youth you really do understand the Way of chess. You combine the Zen and the Taoist schools and you are brilliant at seizing your opportunities and making plans. You know how to seize the initiative through a display of strength and also how to win by letting your opponent attack

家後人,這次「出山」玩玩兒棋,不想就奪了頭把交椅,評了這次比賽的大勢,直歎棋道不興。老者看完了棋,輕輕抻一抻衣衫,跺一跺土,昂了頭,由人攙進棋場。眾人都一擁而起。我急忙搶進了大門,跟在後面。只見老者進了大門,立定,往前看去。

王一生孤身一人坐在大屋子中央,瞪眼看着我們,雙手支在膝上,鐵鑄一個細樹樁,似無所見,似無所聞。高高的一盞電燈,暗暗地照在他臉上,眼睛深陷進去,黑黑的似俯視大千世界,茫茫宇宙。那生命像聚在一頭亂髮中,久久不散,又慢慢瀰漫開來,灼得人臉熱。

眾人都呆了,都不說話。外面傳了半天,眼前卻是一個瘦小黑魂,靜靜地坐着,眾人都不禁吸了一口涼氣。

半晌,老者咳嗽一下,底氣很足,十分洪亮,在屋裏蕩來蕩去。王一生忽然目光短了,發覺了眾人,輕輕地掙了一下,卻動不了。老者推開攙的人,向前邁了幾步,立定,雙手合在腹前摩挲了一下,朗聲叫道:「後生,老朽身有不便,不能親赴沙場。命人傳棋,實出無奈。你小小年紀,就有這般棋道,我看了,匯道禪於一

first. You can get rid of the dragon and bring the waters under control, and combine the positive and the negative. That is all the great players of ancient and modern times have had at their disposal. I am lucky to have encountered you in my declining years. I've been deeply moved. China's chess is not finished after all. Will you give me your friendship despite the difference in our ages? I have played this game for fun. Would you be willing to settle for a draw and leave me a little face?"

Wang Yisheng tried and failed again to get up. Legballs and I rushed over to him and helped him to his feet by lifting him under the armpits. His feet hung in mid-air bent in a sitting posture and could not be straightened. I felt as if the weight I was lifting was only a few pounds, so I gave Legballs a sign to put Wang Yisheng down and massage his legs. Everyone crowded round. The old man shook his head and sighed. Legballs rubbed Wang Yisheng's body, face and neck gently and firmly with his big hands. After a while Wang Yisheng's body relaxed and he leant against our hands, his throat rasping. Slowly he opened his mouth, closed it, opened it again and groaned. It was a long time before he gasped out, "Call it a draw."

"Won't you eat at my place tonight?" the old man asked with great emotion. "Will you stay on for a couple of days so that we can talk about chess?" "No," said Wang Yisheng quietly with a shake of his head. "I'm with friends. We all set out together and we're going to stick together. We're going to the cultural centre. I've got a friend there." "Let's go," said the painter from the middle of the crowd. "Let's go to my place. I've bought some food. You can all come. It's a rare chance." The others were packed all round us as we slowly pushed our way out. We were lit up by a ring of blazing torches. We were surrounded many times over by mountain folk and people from the district capital, who all struggled to catch a glimpse of the chess master's elegant bearing then nodded and sighed.

爐，神機妙算，先聲有勢，後發制人，遣龍治水，氣貫陰陽，古今儒將，不過如此。老朽有幸與你接手，感觸不少，中華棋道，畢竟不頹，願與你做個忘年之交。老朽這盤棋下到這裏，權做賞玩，不知你可願意平手言和，給老朽一點面子？」

王一生再掙了一下，仍起不來。我和腳卵急忙過去，托住他的腋下，提他起來。他的腿仍然是坐着的樣子，直不了，半空懸着。我感到手裏好像只有幾斤的分量，就示意腳卵把王一生放下，用手去揉他的雙腿。大家都擁過來，老者搖頭歎息着。腳卵用大手在王一生身上、臉上、脖子上緩緩地用力揉。半晌，王一生的身子軟下來，靠在我們手上，喉嚨嘶嘶地響着，慢慢把嘴張開，又合上，再張開，「啊啊」着。很久，才嗚嗚地說：「和了吧。」

老者很感動的樣子，說：「今晚你是不是就在我那兒歇了？養息兩天，我們談談棋？」王一生搖搖頭，輕輕地說：「不了，我還有朋友。大家一起出來的，還是大家在一起吧。我們到、到文化館去，那裏有個朋友。」畫家就在人群裏喊：「走吧，到我那裏去，我已經買好了吃的，你們幾個一起去。真不容易啊。」大家慢慢擁了我們出來，火把一圈兒照着。山民和地區的人層層圍了，爭睹棋王丰采，又都點頭兒歎息。

Slowly I helped Wang Yisheng along, and the light came with us all the way. We went into the cultural centre and on to the painter's room, and although people tried to persuade them to go away, the windows were packed with onlookers. This made the painter so anxious that he put some of his pictures away.

Gradually the crowd dispersed, but Wang Yisheng remained rather numb. Suddenly realising that I was still clutching that chess piece in my left hand I held it out to show Wang Yisheng. At first he gazed at it stupidly, appearing not to recognise it, but then there was a noise in his throat and he brought up something viscous with a violent retching sound. He started weeping and saying through his sobs, "Mum, I've understood now. You've got to have something before you can really live. Mum—" We all felt upset. We swept the floor, fetched him some hot water, and tried to calm him. After crying and getting those pent-up emotions off his chest, Wang Yisheng bucked up again and ate with the rest of us. The painter finally got himself blind drunk, lay down on his wooden bed and went to sleep, ignoring us all. The electrician took us all, including Legballs, to go to sleep on the auditorium stage.

The night was so dark you could not see your hand in front of your face. Wang Yisheng was already sound asleep. I still seemed to hear the hubbub of voices and see everything lit up with blazing torches as the stern-faced mountain folk walked through the forests with firewood on their shoulders, singing their songs. I smiled and thought that only by being one of the common people would one enjoy such pleasures. My family had been destroyed, I had lost my privileged status and was now having to do manual work every day, but here there was a remarkable man who I was very lucky indeed to know. Food and clothing were the basic things, and ever since the human race had existed they have been kept busy every day for them. But it was not really human to be limited to them. I was being gradually overcome by tiredness, so I wrapped myself up in the curtain and fell fast asleep.

我攙了王一生慢慢走,光亮一直隨着。進了文化館,到了畫家的屋子,雖然有人幫着勸散,窗上還是擠滿了人,慌得畫家急忙把一些畫兒藏了。

人漸漸散了,王一生還有些木。我忽然覺出左手還攥着那個棋子,就張了手給王一生看。王一生呆呆地盯着,似乎不認得,可喉嚨裏就有了響聲,猛然「哇」地一聲兒吐出一些粘液,嗚嗚地説:「媽,兒今天……媽──」大家都有些酸,掃了地下,打來水,勸了。王一生哭過,滯氣調理過來,有了精神,就一起吃飯。畫家竟喝得大醉,也不管大家,一個倒在木牀上睡去。電工領了我們,腳卵也跟着,一齊到禮堂台上去睡。

夜黑黑的,伸手不見五指。王一生已經睡死。我卻還似乎耳邊人聲嚷動,眼前火把通明,山民們鐵了臉,捎着柴禾在林中走,咿咿呀呀地唱。我笑起來,想:不做俗人,哪兒會知道這般樂趣?家破人夭,平了頭每日荷鋤,卻自有真人生在裏面,識到了,即是幸,即是福。衣食是本,自有人類,就是每日在忙這個。可囿在其中,終於還不太像人。倦意漸漸上來,就攏了幕布,沉沉睡去。